During and after the last war Ted Allbeury served as an officer in the Intelligence Corps, working on counter-intelligence duties. Since then he has been a director of an advertising agency, a farmer, managing director of a pirate radio station, and a PR consultant. He now lives in Lamberhurst. Kent, with his family.

By the same author

TED ALLBEURY

Moscow Quadrille

GRANADA
London Toronto Sydney New York

Published by Granada Publishing Limited in 1978
Reprinted 1978, 1983

ISBN 0 583 12784 3

First published in Great Britain by
Peter Davies Ltd 1976
Copyright © Ted Allbeury 1976

Granada Publishing Limited
Frogmore, St Albans, Herts AL2 2NF
and
36 Golden Square, London W1R 4AH
515 Madison Avenue, New York, NY 10022, USA
117 York Street, Sydney, NSW 2000, Australia
60 International Blvd, Rexdale, Ontario, R9W 6J2, Canada
61 Beach Road, Auckland, New Zealand

Printed and bound by
Richard Clay (The Chaucer Press) Ltd,
Bungay, Suffolk

Granada ®
Granada Publishing ®

To past and present members
of the Special Forces Club, London,
and to all those members of S O E
whose courage was so singularly ignored
when it was all over.

PART ONE

CHAPTER ONE

There were bright red poppies wherever you looked in the cornfield, and alongside the path there were white and blue cornflowers. It was only thirty kilometers from the centre of Moscow, and less than ten from the outer ring road. They had sat together on the headland where the beech trees and elms stood in a cluster at the corner of the field. The girl was wearing a summer dress. Pale biscuit coloured with white edging. The skirt was long and loose but had been pulled up to her hips, and the white buttons on the bodice were undone so that she was naked to the waist. As his hands fondled her breasts she was drinking vodka from a bottle.

Her head was back and the thick, long, blonde hair was like straw-coloured silk as it cascaded past her shoulders. Although she was almost twenty her pretty face had a sort of schoolgirl innocence, an apparent lack of awareness of her beauty and her attraction. The big blue eyes were almost closed against the sun, and the long lashes cast a soft shadow on her cheeks. The small neat nose was perfect, even if the soft red mouth could be considered too big. As she swallowed, the stem of her throat pulsed like a blackbird's when it sings. Krasin looked at her and wondered how this young beauty had been born to such plain and humble parents. The father had died five years earlier, and the photographs had shown a typical clerk's face. Her mother could only have given the genes for the beautiful blue eyes and the magnificent breasts.

With a final gulp she finished the vodka and one shapely, rounded arm drew back as she flung the bottle in a curving arc so that it fell into the waving corn. She turned to look at his face and then her eyes went down to watch his hands as they kneaded her breasts. She watched for a few moments

9

and then looked back at his face. He was much more than twice her age. A handsome man in a world-beaten sort of way. Pouchy eyes that always looked amused, or ready to be amused. A full, firm mouth and chin, and, despite a receding hair-line, his wavy hair was at least as much black as grey. She had once seen a film with an English star named Rex Harrison who could have been his double. And Viktor Krasin had that same indestuctible charm.

Because of the heat of the sun and the effect of the vodka she lay back on the warm earth and left him to his simple enjoyment. Since she was fifteen, men had wanted her body, and for small favours and small presents she had let them have their way. She had never responded emotionally but that had not been a hindrance. But Krasin had sometimes seemed to care. From time to time he took her into Moscow, and she watched him perform at the theatres, or on television or radio. He took her to parties, and although he adopted no proprietary air, she turned aside the other Moscow propositions that came her way. She could never be independent of him in Moscow, because she had no Residence Permit, and that meant she could not rent a room or stay overnight except with him. But it had been Krasin who had fixed for her to attend the junior acting school, and it had been Krasin who softened the blow when after two terms they had thrown her out. They had been firm in their opinion that she was quite unsuitable on the grounds of instability of temperament. But as Krasin had emphasized, she had come out with a formal grace added to her natural animal litheness, and an exceptional talent for French and English.

Even with her eyes closed she could see the orange disc of the sun. It reminded her of a picture she had seen on a wall in Krasin's apartment. It was a print of a painting by a man who signed his name as Vincent, and he'd made the sun look like a big yellow flower.

It was almost an hour later when he had walked her back to the village, and after drinking tea with the family he had motored off to Moscow. He reminded her to listen to him on

Radio Moscow that evening. They were doing *Uncle Vanya* again.

Although he was in his early fifties he had one of those neat Scottish faces that look perennially young. The red hair went with the pink cheeks, the blue eyes, the freckles and the neat moustache. Sir James Hoult sat on the edge of the double bed looking through Hardy's new catalogue. He wanted one of the new pattern spinning rods but he didn't like the look of the prices. He closed the book and laid it beside him on the bed. Maybe next leave he'd make the trip to Alnwick and see if he could drive a bit of a bargain.

He stood up and walked to the mirror to tie the black tie. A few minutes later he was easing on his jacket. Without his shoes he was a little short for the mirror, but not so short that he couldn't see the two rows of pretty ribbons that started with the DSO and ended with the General Service Medal. He was always surprised at how much the Russians loved the fancy dress bit, and the medals and decorations. Not that he didn't agree with them about the medals. For Sir James, the world divided quickly and easily into those who had served in World War II, and those who had 'skulked' at home.

He was tying his shoe-laces when his wife came into their room. She was long ago ready for the fray and as she swept across the rooms picking up his clothes she said, without pausing, 'Don't put your shoes on the bed, Jamie.' He looked up and across at her and saw that she was smiling.

'I wish I'd known you when you wore a uniform, Jamie. You must have looked very chic in a kilt.'

She sat down on one of the embroidered chairs. Adèle de Massu made a very elegant ambassador's wife, and His Excellency knew that if it were not for her his time in Moscow would have set a new low for the social niceties. If you grew up in the sharp social atmosphere of a house in the Avenue Foch and a château on the Loire, then the embassy in Moscow was child's play.

11

She was searching through her linen handbag and he looked at her with smiling affection. For all the airs and graces she was only a grown-up girl doing what *maman* had always done. The light shone on the black hair as it swept to a chignon, revealing the childlike, gentle neck and the white, sloping shoulders. She looked up and caught him smiling.

'Tell me why you're smiling?'

'Because you're beautiful.'

She shook her head. 'That's a diplomat's answer. The truth will be plainer but nicer.'

He nodded as he looked back at her. 'You're right, as always. You look like a very young girl getting ready for her first party.'

The brown eyes gazed back at him for a few seconds and then she said softly, 'You know, you're a very perceptive man.' And she walked over and tucked her arm in his as they walked to the door. She liked this man, apart from loving him, he had wisdom and resources to spare. They all said he was the toughest Scot in a very tough bunch, but she knew better. He ought to have been a priest, not a soldier, and never a diplomat.

The KGB lieutenant was watching the control panel. It was a few minutes before midnight. There were six tape-recorders laid out on the bench. They were Revox A77 Mk IVs with extra-large spools. All the recorders were live but only two of them were moving, and their tapes wound slowly past the recording heads on to the take-up spools. From time to time they stopped, and then as the solenoids clicked they would start again. The solenoids were activated by sounds from the hidden microphones in the embassy. Number 3 was recording a conversation in the Trade Attaché's office with a visiting businessman. He had been to the reception at the French Embassy with the senior British Embassy staff, and now he was asking where the action was in Moscow's night-life. He was getting the standard warnings. On number 5 the Ambassador was dictating notes to his secretary about the conversation and gossip that had taken place at the reception. The secretary was new, and there had been much argument among the English-speaking team as to her accent. It had been settled eventually by the Professor of Phonetics at Leningrad University. She was from somewhere near Birmingham. But he had had to use oscilloscope traces before he could make the final pronouncement.

Like all the other embassies the British Embassy was monitored on a 24-hour basis, but normally the responsibility was Section III's. But for four weeks the responsibility had been transferred to Section I, and a special English-speaking team had been seconded to the operation. There had been no hint of what it was all about.

There was a front-page piece with a photograph in the *Kent Messenger*. It showed Piers Hoult, the elder son of Sir James Hoult, presenting the blue registration book of a 12-metre fibre-glass twin-engined cruiser to the leader of Medway Sea Scouts. The report said that the boat had been presented by the Soviet Trade Mission to Sir James for his help in arranging distribution of the Soviet-built craft in Great Britain. He in turn had presented it to the Sea Scouts who were obviously delighted.

Although the main KGB complex had moved to the massive new building on the outer ring road, the old HQ at Dzerzhinsky Square was still used from time to time by the top brass. The old hands preferred it, especially for meetings.

The room was a mixture of Empire and William Morris, with a deep red, flock wallpaper, and beautiful tall, narrow windows. The shutters had been fastened back and the autumn breeze was gently flapping the hems of the long net curtains. At one end of the room was a massive stone fireplace and a circular table, set with bowls of fruit and nuts. There were eight comfortable leather chairs set around the table, and above the mantelpiece an old poster of Lenin, framed in maplewood. At the other end of the room was a long mahogany table, polished like glass, and set for five

13

places with paper and pencils.

Four men were already sitting at the table and the one who was making notes looked up as the door opened, nodded at the late-comer, and went back to his writing. He sensed that the other three were annoyed at the man's late arrival but he felt no annoyance himself. After all, it was typical Krasin. Typical actor. The late entrance probably gave him a sense of importance, an air of condescension. A few moments later he put down his pencil and shifted the files to one side. He looked up and glanced quickly around the others at the table.

'There's tea and coffee on the back table, and fruit and so on. Help yourselves as you need. Notes may be taken but they go in the shredder before we leave. The subject of this meeting is of absolute secrecy.'

He didn't look around the table for agreement. He didn't need to. Colonel Soloviev was that sort of man. He rolled the pencil a couple of times up and down the green file cover and then pushed it to one side as he leaned back in his chair. His head went back, resting against the chair, and his eyes closed as if he were trying to exclude some outside distractions from his thoughts. He spoke with a clipped Georgian accent.

'About eight weeks ago we had a report from our London Embassy. The main point of it was that the British Ambassador to Moscow would be recalled to London in about eight months' time.' He opened his eyes and leaned forward, his arms on the table.

'That's six months from now. This report from our London people is also supported by a conversation that Gromyko had at the British Embassy in Paris two weeks ago. They were trying out a name on him. Their proposal for the new ambassador. A perfectly acceptable man by the way. Gromyko said the usual complimentary things about the present ambassador and it was strongly hinted that His Excellency was to have a new function, not just a new posting. It seems that he's to be personal adviser to the Prime Minister on foreign affairs.' He paused to let the silence

14

underline what he had said. Then he continued. 'We should like that man to be on our side. We have six months to make this possible and that is why I have called this meeting. Let me tell you the background that we know.'

He pulled over the files and eased out the thickest. He read for a few moments and then said, 'Right. The basics. His name is Sir James Fletcher Hoult. Born 1920. Educated at Manchester Grammar School. Moderate academic performance. Served in Scottish infantry regiment for six years 1939–45. Demobilized with rank of major. Had several senior posts in the Control Commission in Hanover. Transferred to Foreign Office as special adviser on Western Europe. No family money. Married French woman Adèle de Massu, daughter of wealthy and influential financier. On marrying he joined a London Merchant Bank to advise on European investments for the bank and its clients. Appointed to the Soviet Union as British Ambassador two and a half years ago.' He looked up and leaned back. 'Those are very brief details. There is a five-page report on him that you can read later. I'd like to hear what Viktor has to tell us.' He waved his arm towards Krasin, who half smiled as the others waited on his views. His dual role gave him enough edge to play things a little his own way.

'I know them both well, Aleksander. She's a sweetie, no doubt about that. Genuinely interested in the arts – theatre, painting, poetry – the whole thing. And she's very, very attractive. As for him, well I'd say he doesn't hate us and he doesn't love us. I'd like to see some of his reports to London but I should guess he goes straight down the middle.'

Soloviev nodded and looked across at the man sitting opposite. 'Read us the secondary background notes, Sergei.'

Sergei Kuznetsov never liked this part where facts were left behind and opinion and conjecture took over. He looked over the top of his glasses at Krasin and then Soloviev, and finally bent his head to his papers.

'Firstly the question of the new appointment. We have received in the last fourteen days photocopies of instructions from the Department of the Environment to outside contractors for modifications and redecoration to the Prime Minister's secretaries' office. It has every indication of being converted for the use of a very senior member of the Prime Minister's staff. The completion date is next February. That fits the date we have been given concerning His Excellency.

'His Excellency has never been a member of any political party, but he has been a personal friend of the Prime Minister since school-days. Except for Sir James's war service they have always kept in close touch. We have had many reports that the Prime Minister has frequently sought Hoult's advice on both internal and external affairs. Despite this relationship he is not particularly sympathetic to the Prime Minister's party. In fact there are many reports of very sharp comments by Hoult on both the leading parties. But there is no doubt that it was at the Prime Minister's insistence that he was appointed Ambassador to Moscow. The career diplomats and the civil servants didn't like it at all.

'The regiment he served in is called the Black Watch. A Scottish regiment that wears a pleated skirt. We have pictures on file of uniforms, and of Hoult when he was an officer.

'We have no records of any hobbies, or any sports, and no information regarding sexual activity outside his marriage.'

He put down his papers and pushed his glasses up his forehead. 'We have checked on his finances. He has an account at a Tunbridge Wells branch of Barclays Bank. Four days ago his deposit account stood at seven thousand four hundred pounds. Current account seven hundred and ten pounds. He has a house in a village just outside Tunbridge Wells which has been valued at thirty-five thousand pounds. At the house there is a full-time house-keeper and a part-time gardener. He will be entitled to a pension when he retires of seven thousand pounds a year, at today's values.'

16

He paused, and looked at Soloviev, who said nothing. Krasin spoke without turning towards his companions.

'Have we tried any money games, Soloviev?'

Soloviev half-smiled and nodded.

'Of course. We gave madame a camera for her first birthday in Moscow, a gold watch last Revolution Day, and a valuable ikon for her last birthday. Our people in London did a check. All the gifts had been put on the Foreign Office register. The same applied to all the official and unofficial gifts presented to His Excellency.

'We asked him to use his good offices to help our London Trade Mission launch the new 12-metre power cruiser in Great Britain. We arranged for one to be registered in his name and we paid for a three-year mooring for the boat on the Medway. He made it public very graciously, and handed it over to the local youth movement in Chatham.

'There were a few more things, but I can say quite definitely all the signs are that money will not get him. He's very careful and cautious.'

Krasin nodded. 'That's what I would have said. And he's not homosexual, I can tell you that. I can tell them a mile off, even the secret ones.' He brushed an imaginary speck from his sleeve and then looked straight at Soloviev.

'You'd better put us really in the picture, Aleksander, or we shall wander all over the place.'

Soloviev stood up and walked over to the small table and squeezed the big Comice pears until he found one he fancied. Taking a bite, he walked back to the table. He rested one arm on the back of his chair as he leaned towards the group at the table.

'The Presidium sub-committee want this man to be either well-disposed towards us or under an obligation. They emphasize that it must be done with absolute discretion. We can have whatever resources or funds may be necessary and the operation has highest non-military priority. We are interested in the Ambassador not only because of his influence on the Prime Minister but because of the situation in Britain at the moment.' He shook the pear juice from his hand before he pointed to the fourth man.

'Levin has prepared a detailed evaluation of the political situation in Great Britain but he can give us a résumé good enough for this meeting.'

Soloviev waved his hand at the stocky man in the uniform of a KGB major who nodded and spoke without any reference to notes.

'The views I am giving are those of Special Service Department. It is their considered opinion that Great Britain is now the most Marxist state in Western Europe. This position has been arrived at gradually, but not necessarily at the wish of the people.

'From 1973 we enlarged our influence in the trade unions, the media, and with the politicians. We have maintained a continuous pressure on all these points and the progress made has been extremely satisfactory. Attitudes to worker control, to heavy taxes, to nationalization of companies, to censorship and control of the Press have been changed by subtle legislation and by politicians and the media making it seem acceptable. However we now have small signs of resistance, from Parliament and the people. The voting in the country has stayed fifty-fifty between the two main parties for many years, and that has not altered, but there is growing evidence of a backlash against recent legislation. The Opposition party is gaining support in by-elections and local government elections.

'The Prime Minister has always given the appearance of keeping a balance between his party's right and left wings. The Opposition were disorganized for nearly two years but they are now building support. The Press are muck-raking against the left and it is the department's opinion that in six months' or a year's time the Prime Minister could resign or call an election because of this pressure. We want the Ambassador to hold him steady. We need another eighteen months to two years to consolidate and finalize our gains.'

He looked deliberately at Krasin, the outsider. Krasin pursed his lips and shrugged.

18

'Do the British mean so much to us, comrades?'

It was Soloviev who spoke up quickly.

'They do, my friend. We have big, big, Communist parties in Italy and France. And where does it get us? Nowhere. We have made more progress in London than the rest of Europe put together. We are very near to control of *all* energy, *all* media and *all* transport. Maybe we have no party to talk about but that is not what we work for. We could get control of Great Britain in two months by open revolution, but we should pay a big price for it. We should lose the rest of Europe overnight. If the control comes as it is coming now, quietly and unnoticed, then Europe will go the same way, and like it into the bargain. And all we need is time. Time for the last screws to go in.

'The Ambassador will not be our only weapon, but he could be the decisive one. When weak men, ambitious men, are under pressure, then seemingly neutral advice can tip the scales. We want them to tip our way. The sub-committee have decided that every effort must be made to have this man on our side.'

There were a few moments of silence and then Krasin spoke.

'Do you mean *really* on our side or just under our control?' Soloviev nodded his head in approval. He pointed with a stubby forefinger at the actor.

'Exactly, Viktor, exactly. We should like the first but we accept the second. That must be our concern in this operation. It is why the sub-committee insist on the highest skills being used.' He paused and looked again at Krasin. 'It's why you are here, Viktor. On the one hand we make every effort to persuade this man about our policies but at the same time we take out the insurance of creating an obligation, a pressure point.'

Krasin stood up and stretched his arms. 'There's another piece of insurance we could consider, Aleksander.'

'What's that?'

Krasin turned round smiling. 'Madame herself. She is more pliable, I suspect, than Sir James.'

Soloviev closed his eyes for a moment. His lips were pursed when he opened them again.

'We should have to be very careful. We must not look too active. But you can be the judge of that, my friend.'

Krasin's smile had broadened to a grin. 'I have the feeling that you want me to mount this production.'

Soloviev was wiping his fingers on a fine linen handkerchief and he didn't look up as he spoke.

'That's it, Krasin. Any ideas?'

Krasin folded his long body on to the chair and stretched out his legs alongside the table. His hands were thrust deep in his pockets and his teeth slowly gnawed at his lower lip as he sat thinking. When he spoke, it was slowly and quietly. Almost as if he were speaking aloud to himself.

'It's got to be "the swallows". It's not going to be money, it's not boys, so that only leaves the girls. So what kind of girl? I'd say she's got to be much like his wife. Elegant, educated, independent, with a talent, brunette, and very, very beautiful. Men either want the same again but a younger model, or the complete opposite. I'd say he would go for the same again.'

'So who have you got in mind?'

Krasin for once looked serious. His hands were together as if in prayer, and his fingertips were touching his mouth as he thought. He rocked gently in the chair and his eyes were still, in concentration. They were all silent for long minutes and then the long tapered fingers laced together and locked in decision as Krasin turned towards the others at the table.

'I think it should be Lydia. Lydia Ouspenskaya.'

And he smiled with pleasure at the niceness of his thinking. It was Soloviev who first spoke.

'Is that the girl who was on "Novosti dnya" last week, talking about modern films?'

'That's her. I didn't see that newsreel but she's been used for nearly two years as a liaison when we have been negotiating joint film ventures with the Americans and the British.'

'What joint ventures are these?' Kuznetsov looked entirely disapproving and Krasin enjoyed his opportunity to annoy him further.

'The film of Tchaikovsky was in collaboration with the Americans, and *The Red Tent* was with the British. The male star was British – an actor named Peter Finch.'

'Is this true, Soloviev?'

Soloviev looked annoyed at the question. 'If comrade Krasin says it is, then I am sure he is correct. Films are his business, Sergei.' He turned in dismissal towards Krasin. 'What would she want, Viktor?'

Krasin smiled and shrugged. 'Money, sweet words, and constant approval from all and sundry.'

'She's very beautiful. Is she experienced?'

'You mean in bed, comrade?'

'Yes. And in these sort of matters.'

'Very experienced in bed. Several generals, a handful of diplomats, and half the male leads at Tverskoi Boulevard. As far as this scenario is concerned she would do as I tell her. She would be ideal.'

Soloviev glanced at the others. 'Any objections?'

Nobody spoke. He turned to Krasin.

'Krasin, I want you to handle this. I want it really stage-managed. No false notes. Is that understood?'

CHAPTER TWO

Krasin had sat alone in the room with the files, reading them through with a thoroughness that would have surprised all his colleagues except Soloviev. It was past midnight when he stood at the top of the steps and looked out over the square.

The lights from Red Square were reflected on the low clouds, and as he walked across Sverdlova Place he could see the white front of the Bolshoi Theatre, washed clean by the massive floodlights. There were youngsters standing on the steps, looking at the photographs and programmes in the glass frames. And over to his left, the lights were blazing for the foreigners at the National Hotel. For a moment he felt an urge to be amongst lively people again, but it passed, and he walked up on Gorkovo Ulitsa to the block where he had his two rooms.

He turned the switch and looked around the living-room. He always had the 'loner's' instinct to check his place over before he relaxed. Some day there would be another night of the long knives at the KGB, and he would come home and find that the wrong side had won. The furniture would be smashed and the wallpaper and carpets ripped up from the hurried search, and there would be the melted faces of the thugs from the Fifth Directorate as they smiled and waited for him to turn and flee. But everything was in its place.

He slid off his jacket and walked to the small cupboard. When he had poured himself a whisky he sipped it and placed it on the window alongside the piano. The elegant stool creaked as he sat down, but his eyes were on the golden frame and the gleaming crossed strings of the Blüthner grand.

He wasn't a musician but he could play well enough to

22

amuse himself. He rolled back his sleeves, and his fingers were tentative at first, until the left hand became alive and the little finger splayed sideways for those haunting tenths that so delighted him. As he played lazily through the counterpoint of 'Manhattan' he changed key as he merged into Chaminade's little 'Plaisirs d'Amour', and then something that had a line that went '... le chaland qui passe', but he couldn't remember the next line. He stopped, reached for the whisky, and walked over to the radio. As he switched on they were playing 'Kalinka'. That was the third time he had heard it, at about this time, in the last week. Probably the boys in Department 13 passing codes to some lonely 'illegal' in Paris, Hamburg, or London. The early hours of the morning could produce some pretty odd programming.

He reached for his address book, checked a number and dialled. He hung on for three or four minutes but there was no reply. She must be with the blond major-general. What the hell was his name? Began with an S. Something like Simonov. Sinyovsky, that was it, Andrei Sinyovsky. A pompous bastard, old enough to be her grandfather but hadn't made it beyond major-general. He checked Sinyovsky's number with HQ Moscow Central Defence, and dialled. It rang for a long time before a man's hoarse voice answered.

'Sinyovsky. Who is that?'

'I want to speak to Lydia Ouspenskaya, comrade general.'

'Who the hell is that?'

Krasin smiled to himself, but he said nothing. The general spoke again. 'I said who is that?'

'I want to speak to Ouspenskaya.'

There was a short silence and then a slightly cautious voice said, 'She is not available.'

Krasin smiled. All you had to do with the military gorillas was dig a nice hole and wait for them to fall in.

'I see, well just ask her what the number of her Moscow Residence Permit is, will you.'

There was some heavy breathing at the other end and

23

then the honeyed bedroom voice of the girl.

'Lydia Ouspenskaya here. Who is that?'

'It's Krasin, my dear. I want you round at my place.'

'Now?'

'Now.'

'But it's nearly half past two, Viktor.'

'So?'

'Where is Yelena, Viktor? Have you quarrelled?'

Krasin sighed. 'Lydia. This is official. Just get dressed and come over. Tell him to drop you outside and then you come straight up. Press my bell and I'll release the small door on the left.' And he hung up.

Even at that time in the morning she looked chic and composed. The black suit with the braid trimmings was obviously Paris, as was the pale, pale, pink chiffon scarf at her neck. Her face was entirely Russian but only the high cheeks made its beauty anything other than international. The cool high forehead, the fine, perfect nose, the large, deep brown eyes all gave to her face a glowing beauty that only emphasized the calm, well-shaped mouth that gave at each corner to deep dimples, even when she wasn't smiling. She sat with her long legs in smooth tan nylons that flowed down to the neat black shoes where her small feet were pressed together like the prim neat paws of some pretty cat. The black hair was swept back to a ribboned tail at the nape of her neck, but despite its smooth sleekness it looked elegant rather than severe.

She shook her head when Krasin offered her a cigarette. She was impatient to know what it was all about. The KGB called its panel of girls for seducing foreigners, the swallows. Lydia Ouspenskaya was a 'swallow', but she was infrequently used. She had talents apart from her good looks and her body. They only used her on very special occasions and her casual but continuous relationship with Krasin was based on a mixture of both her areas of skill. She classed him as a friend, and within the usual limits of Moscow life, she trusted him. Like many of the more

24

sophisticated women in Moscow, she found him attractive, both mentally and physically. There were hundreds of attractive men in Moscow, but Krasin was unique. He seemed indifferent to the official pressures, and had a charmed life in avoiding those clashes that seemed inevitable among the top brass of the Party, and at all levels of the KGB. The foreigners loved him, and saw him as one of themselves. But on this she knew they were wrong. Behind the charm, away from the genuine talent as an actor, there was a hard, unflinching dedication to the Party line. He may make the wittiest jokes against the Moscow top brass, and he may never disclose the names of those who laughed loudest, but that was only because he deemed them too insignificant to manoeuvre in his class. He was like a shark among minnows.

She had had sex with him twice, and although there was nothing she could put it down to, she was left with the feeling that it was solely research. There was no doubt that he had enjoyed her, but the first time she was sure that it was a kind of exploration, and the second time, it was as if he were checking out one or two points from their first encounter. To make sure that the first time had not been atypical. She had not felt that she had learned anything about Krasin's own sexual tastes. There had been enthusiasm for everything, but she had noticed that even when he climaxed his eyes had been open and they had been watching her.

And now he had spent over an hour outlining the objectives of his plan, and had coached her in the type of approach that she should use. She had not been told why the Ambassador was so important, or what would happen when she had achieved a relationship with him.

Krasin was arranging a Moscow Residence Permit for her and a small apartment just off Mayakovsky Square. An account was opened in her name at the KGB pay-office in the Council of Ministers building inside the Kremlin. She was given a simple word code to use on the telephone, and two telephone numbers. One was for routine contact, and the other for immediate assistance or instructions.

For the next three days Krasin had listened to the accumulated hours of recordings of the small talk of the Embassy. He had had long conversations with two of the embassy maids and the chauffeur. By the end of the week he had worked out a careful timetable. He had also set up a team to work on one of the English secretaries, and another to test out the Trade Attaché. By that time Lydia Ouspenskaya had attended two diplomatic functions which had also been attended by the Ambassador. On Krasin's instructions she had made no attempt at a direct contact.

In the middle of the following week Sir James and his wife had been invited to a Kremlin cocktail party given by the Ministry of Culture. Along with half a dozen others, Lydia Ouspenskaya had been introduced to Their Excellencies. Krasin had been there and he had watched the Ambassador's reactions. Apart from formal politeness there had been none.

All the embassy servants painted a picture of an amiable marriage, with the wife maintaining the social graces and the husband going along with a social scene to which he was completely indifferent. In the first month Krasin, Lydia and sometimes Yelena had been in the Ambassador's company two or three times a week. Lydia had been only one of several pretty girls in the Krasin circle and it wasn't until week six that she had been with the Ambassador, even for a few moments, away from the others.

It was one of those nights with rich blue skies and stars that crackled with the first cold of autumn. The massive floodlights lit up the big pitch and the front of the stands, so that in the darkness the crowds were invisible, except where a match flared to light a pipe or a cigarette. There was the usual big crowd despite the fact that it was only a friendly game, and behind the east-side goal there were the blue banners of Scotland, lurching and waving, as willing but unsteady arms held them high. Glasgow Rangers were playing Moscow Dynamo in the first international friendly before the season proper began.

The party in the VIPs' box were all men except for Lydia and Yelena. Lydia sat between the Ambassador and Krasin, and on the other side of Krasin was Yelena. Lydia's lovely face was set in a cloud of silver fox and the cold had put an apple glow on her cheeks and the same star sparkle in her eyes. At half-time the game was still a goalless draw but Lydia had wanted to go down and meet the visiting team. Krasin and the Ambassador were persuasive, so she agreed that she would wait until the match was over. When the whistle finally blew the home team had scored a couple of goals, and the crowd had been well pleased. The Ambassador saw the police arresting some of his compatriots who were streaming across the pitch, scarves waving aloft, bottles in hand.

The President of the Scottish Football Association had walked them both down to the dressing room. Through the steam and the stench of liniment they had shaken hands with towel-draped players, and despite Lydia Ouspenskaya's excellent English she had barely understood a word. When they walked out of the dressing room Krasin was awaiting them with Yelena and a man in uniform. Rather than imprison the Scottish supporters the deputy head of Moscow's police thought that a sharp word from the Ambassador would suffice.

The big cell was at the other side of the stadium and the noise was considerable as they approached the Rangers' supporters. There was the stench of vomit in the corridor, and Sir James had motioned to the girls to wait with Krasin as he walked towards the open door of the cell. But Krasin had ignored the gesture and they had stood just behind the Scot as he faced his fellow countrymen. They knew what a Russian would do, and they wondered what the Scot would do.

He stood in the door and the room gradually became silent as he looked at all the faces. They were Black Watch

27

faces, Highland Light Infantry faces, and he knew them from way, way back. When the silence was complete, he spoke.

'Good evening gentlemen. My name is Hoult. Jamie Hoult. I'm your Ambassador here in Moscow and I'm glad to see you all. It was a grand game and a fair result. And I'm awfu' glad you made the journey. I've come along to wish ya' all a guid journey home. There's no' many of us Scots in this city tonight, so be guid, guid laddies.' He half turned to go, and then turned back towards them again.

'You'll recall what our wee man once said.

> "A man may fight and no be drunk;
> A man may fight and no be slain;
> A man may kiss a bonnie lass,
> And aye be welcome back again." '

There was a moment's silence then a roar of approval and the stiff, neat man walked round to shake hands with his motley crew.

The Russians had only vaguely understood what was going on, but they knew they'd seen a professional at work.

The four of them had gone back to Krasin's place to celebrate and His Excellency had toasted the Dynamo team and their victory. It was Yelena who had asked the grating question.

'Do all Scotsmen get drunk like that?'

His Excellency had put down his glass and looked across at the girl. He thought for a moment, and then with his head slightly on one side, as if he were listening too, he said very slowly, as he looked at her, 'When you work shamefully hard for very little money, when you cannot read or write, and you live in filthy conditions, you get drunk or you start a revolution.' He smilted faintly as he went on, 'And who is to say which is the better solution?'

It was Krasin who had broken the silence.

'Was it a poem that you said to them?'

Hoult nodded. 'Aye it was. It was by Robert Burns, your

favourite here in Moscow.'

'Tell us about him.' It was the smiling Lydia who finally got him talking.

It was two hours later when they phoned for the embassy car and His Excellency had dropped Lydia Ouspenskaya at the door of her apartment building.

During the next week Krasin had kept Lydia away from the social scene, but he had arranged for Adèle Hoult to be the principal guest of Gromyko and his wife at the Bolshoi, for a special performance of Vainonen's 'Flames of Paris'. The Ambassador was away in Leningrad for two days with the Naval Attaché.

Krasin had driven her ladyship back to the Embassy himself, and they'd talked music till the early hours of the morning. He wasn't foolish enough to mistake her mild flirting for anything more than diplomatic routine. But he was aware that she listened attentively, and played the hostess, a shade beyond what was basic.

Early the following week there had been a trip on the river for the ladies of the French and British embassies, and Krasin had played host with charm, in both languages. There had been a present for everyone. Black Russian tea with lemon and a spoonful of blackcurrant jelly had been served for a toast to the ladies at the noonday picnic. The tall drinking glasses were in graceful silver holders, and when these had been washed and dried, the holders had been engraved by two craftsmen while the ladies were visiting the rose gardens at Gorky Park. Each gift had been wrapped in tissue paper and tied with pink ribbon.

When Adèle Hoult unwrapped hers that evening she had smiled at the inscription. – 'Belle dame – bel jour. Moscou.'

There was a small ceremony the following week in Leningrad. The Hermitage Museum was lending six of its French impressionists to the Royal Academy and the Director had invited the Ambassador to inspect the gallery before the paintings were removed, take tea with the museum's curators and be interviewed on TV.

For once there were none of the old familiar faces. Everyone was a stranger. But when the formalities were almost over a TV crew had started setting up their lights and equipment and Lydia Ouspenskaya had come walking across the great hall with an entourage of young men and a clipboard under her arm. He had felt suddenly glad to see that charming smile, and his tension had slid away. He was with old friends again, and could relax. The formalities concerning the paintings behind them, she had led him into talking about himself, and his life in Moscow. When the lights had been switched off he realized that for the first time in his life he had enjoyed taking part in a TV interview.

They had motored back to Moscow together, and it was midnight when they drew up at her flat.

Krasin had listened intently to the phone message but he had asked no questions. He knew that the girl would report to him as soon as she could. She had arrived half an hour later. When she was settled in the comfortable armchair, he had poured her a drink, and sat down opposite her.

'They tell me you did well today.' His smile was amused.

'You mean you've got a team there permanently?'

'Of course.'

'I've never heard a thing, or seen a thing.'

He laughed. 'You're not supposed to, my dear. Tell me what happened.'

She smiled. 'Didn't they tell you? Didn't they play you the tapes?'

'I want you to tell me.'

'There wasn't very much, Viktor, really. A few kisses and a wandering hand.'

'Go on.'

'Your scheme worked well. I think he was glad to see me in Leningrad. There was nobody else that he knew. He took me to dinner at the Metropol and then he walked with me in Lenin Park. We went to the wide-screen movie and saw that travel thing. He seemed to enjoy it, being with

people I mean. He's a simple man behind all the protocol.
Then he drove me back to Moscow in his official car and I
invited him in for a coffee and that was that.'

'How did you get him going?'

'I didn't really. Although I suppose I did in a way. I
asked him about that Scottish poet and he said some of
the poems for me. And then he said a very nice love poem
about a red rose and he kissed me. And so on.'

'Where did this happen?'

'In the living-room.'

'Where exactly?'

She sighed and then smiled rather ruefully.

'I was leaning against the door.'

'And he?'

'And he was leaning against me.'

'Was he aroused?'

'Oh yes.'

'And what did he do?'

'He touched me.'

'Your breasts?'

'No. Does it matter, Viktor? He wanted me. Isn't that
enough?'

'Did you encourage him?'

'No. I didn't encourage or discourage. I just didn't stop
him, that's all.'

'Was he satisfied?'

She looked across at him with a touch of impatience.
'Yes. I touched him too.'

'Had he been drinking at all? What did he drink at tea-
time and at dinner?'

'Almost nothing. Nothing but tea at the Hermitage and
about two glasses of wine during dinner.'

'Did you arrange to see him again?'

'No. But he is going to telephone me tomorrow.'

The next day Krasin had listened to the tapes and looked
at the film. It was much as the girl had described and from
past experience he reckoned that it would develop as he

31

had planned.

He phoned the girl late in the morning.

'Has he called you yet?'

'No.'

'I think he will be very cautious on the telephone. He knows the score, so play it very, very, cool. But agree with whatever he says. If you can't contact me before you see him again, let me tell you now that I want you to get him in the bedroom. It's too dark in the other room. And I want him fully committed next time. You understand?'

'I understand, Viktor.' And she had hung up.

He had listened to Hoult's telephone conversation with the girl that evening in the control room, as it took place.

She had been sitting watching the puppet play at the open-air theatre for almost ten minutes before he joined her. Izmailovo Park covers almost 3,000 acres with large stretches of pine forest. It was four o'clock when they walked away from the café and the shadows on the springy turf were already long and black.

When they went into the pine woods Krasin held back the surveillance team. It would have been too obvious if they had followed them. He was pleased in a way. It meant that their man was being cautious. He wanted the girl but not so much that he was going to be indiscreet about it.

The man had strolled out alone later from the shadows of the woods. It had been almost dark, and he had walked casually back to the entrance of the park on Narodny Prospekt. The girl had walked to one of the smaller exits and Krasin had phoned her as soon as the team reported that she was back in her apartment.

'So what happened, Lydia?'

'He is committed.'

'What happened?'

'He had me, that is all.'

'Anything unusual?'

'Nothing. It was typical Moscow routine.'

'What's that?'

'I told him the park used to belong to the Romanovs. Good romantic stuff. He listened politely but he obviously hadn't come for that. I didn't time him, but I would guess three minutes' activity.'

Krasin laughed softly. 'Anything else. Any impression you got that was new?'

'I think he is a lonely man. He has no interest at all in a social life. He despises the parties, the functions and the entertainment. I think he is a very enclosed man, he lives inside himself. He enjoys the sex and obviously wants more, but in a way I think having me is almost a kind of revenge on his wife because she likes the social scene.'

'When are you seeing him again?'

'Day after tomorrow. Madame is going to see her mother in Paris for three days.'

'Where are you meeting?'

'Lenin Library. Old manuscripts department at nine o'clock after he has been to a cocktail party at the Egyptian Embassy. I think he will come back here to my place.'

That night the KGB had recorded all the evidence it needed, and Krasin had called a meeting the next day to report the situation.

When he had given them his report Soloviev had nodded his approval, and leaned forward with his elbows on the table.

'Because of the long-term nature of this operation we have been instructed to ignore the usual programme. We shall go through the routine of the indignant husband, Hoult will be brought here to Dzerzhinsky Square, and I will deal with him. There will be no pressure on him at all, we shall be entirely on his side, there will be no hint of a threat, no hint of a deal. We shall just get him off the hook and off he goes. Everything will go on as normal and we shall see that for the rest of his time here he gets VIP treatment at the highest level. Is that understood?'

The others nodded and Soloviev continued.

'It will be you who comes to the rescue, Krasin. You

33

who reassures him. I want this affaire to go on for another six weeks, and then we hit him. I understand that you know the girl's husband so you can do the management of the confrontation. No violence, just abuse, so that we establish that a legal offence has been committed. You clear with me in six weeks' time, say about New Year's Day. You got that?'

'Sure. I'd like the file on her husband.'

Soloviev reached over and pressed the bell. When the lieutenant came in he ordered him to bring Krasin the file.

Krasin read it carefully for an hour.

For three weeks half a dozen pretty girls had made up the team with Krasin, Lydia, Yelena and two young KGB captains. They were part of the crowd at after-theatre parties and diplomatic functions. They didn't start as a homogeneous group, they were sprinkled through guest lists so that the British couple had a wide circle of beautiful and lively people who gradually became an automatic part of their circle.

His Excellency had his sessions once a week with Lydia, and Krasin often sat, after all the other guests had gone, in the drawing-room at the Embassy. The favours that he did for madame were by now far beyond the routine favours that her position would have demanded. There was no doubt that she was genuinely fond of Krasin, but he made no move to put her affection to any physical test.

There were occasions when the British couple, Krasin, Lydia and Yelena, went together on small expeditions to places that were forbidden to the normal run of diplomats. Adèle especially enjoyed going behind the scenes on film lots, and at the ballet and radio. The four of them frequently sat in the control room when Krasin or Lydia was performing on radio or TV. There was soon a tacit understanding that the small circle needed no specific invitations, and Krasin showed the same affection for each of the three ladies. He was theirs to command. His Excellency adopted much the same attitude.

In the week that Soloviev had discussed the coming confrontation, Krasin had flown to Warsaw. Lydia's husband was one of the directors of the film school at Krakow and he needed to be briefed. It was routine that an actual offence should be committed that could lead to prosecution, if only for a possible breach of the peace. And it was routine that the real husband should be used. Foreign security men could check on such things, and if KGB pressure could be proved it meant complications.

They had met at the KGB training school on the outskirts of Warsaw, and the younger man had looked faintly amused as the scenario was explained to him. Lydia and he had gone their own ways for over two years, and he took it for granted that there would be other men. Nikolai Glazunov was a handsome man and he had all the girls he needed, if not all the girls he wanted. He was amused at being cast in the traditional role of the jealous husband.

He sat on the table swinging his long legs as he listened to Krasin. He interrupted.

'I don't have to beat him up or anything ridiculous like that?'

'Of course not. But you've got to be angry. Taking advantage of a man away from home and all that. And a determination to call the police.'

'So who's the lucky man?'

'The Ambassador. The British Ambassador.'

Glazunov shrugged. 'And who is *he* these days?'

'Sir James Hoult.'

The young man's legs stopped swinging and as he looked at Krasin he slid off the table and stood staring at the KGB man's face.

'You must be out of your mind, Viktor. I know him. And I know his wife. They are civilized people. He would see it was a pretence on my part. He knows my views on these things.'

Krasin felt cold with fear, but it barely showed in his voice.

'Where did you know them, Nikolai? When was it?'

The young man laughed uneasily, and with embarrassment.

'I knew them when I was Cultural Attaché in Paris, and he was director of some bank or other, with a branch in Paris. I knew Adèle and her parents years ago when I was at art school in Paris after the war.'

'How well did you know them?'

'Very well indeed. We were good friends for years. Not continually, but wc corresponded regularly.' He turned to Krasin. 'And you say that Jamie Hoult sleeps with Lydia. I can't believe it.'

'Why not?'

'God. I can't say. Lydia's beautiful but she's hard, brittle. Not unlike his Adèle. I suppose that's what it is. Lydia is just a younger version of his wife. But I often used to wonder what went on between those two.'

'What made you wonder?'

Glazunov combed his fingers through his thick blond hair and pursed his lips as he thought. He was frowning as he looked at Krasin.

'Hoult is an odd man you know. Lives a life inside himself. Adèle was tough, but she was naturally gay. He wasn't gay, ever. He went along with it all because of her. I would have guessed not much sex for him, or maybe something odd. Sadism, masochism, something like that. I'm amazed that he's been having sex with Lydia. I wonder if he's resentful of the way Adèle cracks the whip, and he screws Lydia to compensate in some way. You should get one of your psycho boys to do a report on him.'

'We haven't got time now, Niko. It's too late.'

'Why the hell didn't somebody check with me when it all started?'

'God knows. We ought to have done.'

'Find another girl then.'

'There isn't time to establish what we want. We've got to be able to make it stick so that it works after he's gone back to London.'

Domodedovo Airport is probably the largest in the world. It's 30 miles south-east of Moscow on the Kashira Highway. The helicopter had put Krasin down in one of the Red Army's security bays, and he had walked on through to the main terminal building.

He sat with a whisky, looking blankly over the dark airfield. The big, fast jets were landing and taking off for the far corners of the Soviet Union. Peasant families sat in huddles with their woven baskets and cases, and senior-looking officials chatted in small groups, grinding their Ministry axes. For once Krasin was envious. He would gladly have changed places with either the peasants or the bureaucrats. A top-priority KGB operation had crumbled to disaster in one afternoon. Glazunov was able to go back to his work unconcerned, and probably amused at the shambles. Nobody could have planned every detail more carefully than he had, but a stupid, impossible-to-foresee detail, a billion-to-one chance, and the work of dozens of people for months had come to nothing. And it was not just the waste of time and resources. The operation was not repeatable.

He shivered, turned up his coat collar, and walked to the phone booths. He called Lydia, and brusquely told her to contact Yelena. The two of them would go to the country for the night. He'd face the storms in the morning when he had had time to absorb the disaster and work out some sort of defence.

They sat in Lydia's small living-room, Krasin still wearing his coat as he drank a large vodka, and the two girls sitting opposite him on the couch. For nearly an hour they had tried to cheer him up, but they didn't know the cause of his depression. They assumed it was the normal 'ennui' that all creative people suffer from, from time to time. But finally he had stood up and taken off his coat.

Saying it all aloud to somebody would help. So he had told them of his meeting with Glazunov that afternoon in Warsaw, and its disastrous repercussions on the KGB operation. It was Lydia who had responded first.

'Can't you do it with another girl, Viktor?'

'There isn't time, my dear. It's got to be a good enough relationship to be revived in the future.'

'How much time is there? When does he leave?'

'About six or seven weeks. I'm not sure. Has he said anything to you?'

'No. He's not a great talker.'

'Not even in bed?'

She shook her head. 'Especially not in bed. He just has me and that's it. Typical Russian.'

It was Yelena who had thrown the bomb into the desultory conversation. She leaned forward eagerly to Krasin. 'Would I do, Viktor?'

Krasin had smiled and patted her knee.

'There isn't time, my love or I'm sure you'd be first-class.'

'But he likes me.'

Krasin nodded. 'Of course he does, darling. Everybody likes you. You're beautiful.'

'But everybody doesn't say they want me.'

Krasin leaned back in the small chair and stretched out his long legs.

'Then everybody's foolish.'

'He isn't a fool.'

And for the first time Krasin's antennae were alerted. He looked across at the girl.

'What the hell are you saying?'

She shrugged. 'Just that he likes me. He wants me.'

He sat up slowly. 'What makes you think that?'

'He's told me so.'

'What exactly has he said to you, Yelena?'

She frowned and spread her arms as if in despair.

'He talks to me, that is all. He likes me. And he likes my body.'

Krasin's voice was under control but Lydia Ouspenskaya could hear the overtones of anxiety.

'When did he first talk to you?'

'When he went to that restaurant. The Polish one on

38

Oktyabrskaya Square.'

'The Varshava?'

'Yes. That's it.'

'What happened? Was that the night you were drunk?'

'Yes. You were dancing with Lydia, and his wife went over to talk with some Polish Embassy people. He said he wished he was drunk too. He talked about his life. He doesn't like it. He asked me to meet him.'

'Go on.'

'So we meet several times. He gives me presents.'

Krasin looked across at Lydia Ouspenskaya, but her lovely face was impassive.

'Where did you meet?'

'We sometimes go to my house. Twice I met him in Leningrad. The Embassy has a "dacha" near there.'

'What presents has he given you?'

'Flowers, books, money and things like this.'

She pulled down the zip on her dress, and around her neck was a thin gold chain that slid down to where a bright gold sovereign lay between her breasts. It was Lydia Ouspenskaya who broke the silence.

'Why hasn't the surveillance team picked this up, Viktor?'

He shook his head slowly with a half-amused smile. 'Since this operation started the routine surveillance was dropped in case it became too obvious. The surveillance on him has all been on his contacts with you.'

'I think Yelena can save your operation, Viktor.'

He smiled. 'I think maybe you're right, my dear.'

Yelena looked pleased and even Krasin's spirits seemed to be reviving. He stood up.

'Have we got any whisky, Lydia?'

' 'Fraid not, Viktor. His Excellency sometimes brings some, but he drinks it too.'

Krasin looked over at Yelena. 'What did your mother think of the Ambassador?'

'She likes him. He takes his tie off and sits there drinking tea and I have to translate everything they both say.'

'Have you slept with him?'

39

'No.'

'Why not?'

She shrugged and spread her hands. 'I felt there was some sort of arranged thing with Lydia.'

He nodded. 'You'd better stay with Lydia tonight; I'll write out a permit for you and I'll contact you some time tomorrow.'

He wrote out a few lines on the fly-leaf of a book, tore it out, and then signed it.

He walked home slowly through the empty streets and there were tears on his cheeks. He knew now that he cared about Yelena, but he knew that his caring was too late. She was his no longer. Their conversation in Lydia's room would be on the tapes in the adjoining KGB apartment. He had been careful to give nothing of his feelings away, but those who knew him well would be going over the tapes again and again. Looking for a hesitation that was a moment too long, or recognizing with surprise a quaver in his voice that spoke of a dawning disappointment.

Soloviev had listened to Krasin in a frosty silence. It was obvious that he had already been informed of the situation by the surveillance team. When Krasin had finished, Soloviev had not spent time on analysis.

'It is inexcusable, Krasin, that this girl's background had not been thoroughly checked out. Quite inexcusable. It is only accident that leaves us still in the game. This girl Yelena, I understand you know her well.'

'I do, comrade. We have been good friends for nearly two years.'

'Any problems there?'

'Oh yes, plenty of problems.'

Soloviev's head jerked up and his eyes were alert with anger.

'What problems? Tell me.'

'You've met her or seen her, comrade?'

'No. Never.'

'She's just twenty. Very pretty, and very irresponsible.'

'In what way?'

'She drinks too much, and she does not react well to authority.'

'Go on.'

'Just that. She's a peasant, she doesn't seem to be aware of the law, and regulations, and order, and that sort of thing.'

'You mean she's defiant.'

'No. She just doesn't take any notice.'

'Then she must be disciplined.'

'I think that that would be a mistake, comrade colonel. That could ruin what we have left of this operation.'

'Explain.'

'When we were first evaluating what kind of girl he would go for, we said it would either be a younger version of his wife or somebody altogether different. We decided then that somebody like his wife would be most likely to succeed. I think now that we were wrong. I think this girl is what he wants.'

Soloviev looked unimpressed as he looked intently at Krasin's face. His hands went behind his head as he leaned back.

'I should like to hear your reasoning, my friend.'

'Everybody who knows the Ambassador says the same thing. He is a loner, doesn't like the social game, lives inside himself. But we saw how well he dealt with the hooligans at the Dynamo Stadium. He understands that kind of man. He understands peasants because maybe *he's* a peasant under all that camouflage. A very shrewd peasant, but a peasant all the same. He was interested enough in Lydia to sleep with her. So sex still counts with him. But with Yelena it seems it's different. He made the running. And there is at least an elementary relationship beyond just sexual interest. He visits her home, he gives her presents. He *is* interested.'

'Why the hell didn't she tell you about this?'

41

'Why should she? I didn't tell her what was happening. She was part of the scenario, but like most of the others she didn't *need* to know. She obviously sensed that we were trying to please him. She has been part of the scene around Hoult and his wife and she didn't see his interest in her as important.'

Soloviev unfolded his hands from behind his head and groaned his way up till he was standing. He moved his legs to ease the circulation and as he swung his arms he eyed Krasin.

'The Presidium committee have had to be informed about this, and you can take it from me that if it wasn't for your record you would be a long way from Moscow today. So watch your step, Krasin. Watch – every – bloody – step.'

Krasin had had to fight to conceal his anger while he had been briefing Yelena. She didn't react, or when she did, it was with amusement. The only time she had shown any interest was when he had told her that he had fixed a small apartment for her in Moscow. He had promised her a permanent Resident's Permit if the operation was successful.

But she left him uneasy. She hardly seemed to listen, although when he questioned her, it seemed there was nothing she had missed. She was like some pretty child who had learned that her beauty could ward off punishment, and that with charm it could be evaded completely.

She had sat in his apartment with one leg curled beneath her, and her face dutifully raised towards him as he spoke. But she had seemed to concentrate more on gently pulling the petals from a paper sunflower, and arranging them along the arm of the big armchair. The light from the window had put a halo round the blonde hair and warmed the soft cheeks and the tip of her nose. She had looked up and caught his eyes on her breasts, and had smiled with tolerant amusement. They were both aware that her body was no longer his to enjoy. She was special now, with even a KGB registration number, and what was probably the thinnest personal file in the KGB staff records. Her mother was her only living relative.

There was a paragraph in *Pravda*, on page 7, that said that Lydia Ouspenskaya had been flown to a specialist nursing home on the Black Sea so that she could undergo observation for a liver complaint allied to hepatitis. In case nobody believed a word of it, she was shown on her own news programme, waving gently and languidly from a stretcher, as she was lifted up to the doorway of an ambulance plane at Moscow Airport. The camera moved in to a close-up of her lovely face, and then stayed focused on the plane until take-off. If you go that far and people can see the plane leave, it somehow proves that all the story is true. And indeed, the plane flew almost twenty kilometres before it landed at the security airfield at Schelkovo.

Krasin had gone over the contact routine with Yelena again and again. He could have sworn that she didn't even listen, but on test she was absolutely accurate. And then suddenly there was nothing more to say.

She was wearing the same biscuit-coloured dress that she had worn in the field that day and as he looked at her face he had seen her smiling. She knew what he was thinking and she knew that he had cared a little.

Yelena stood on the corner of Karl Marx Boulevard and Pushkin Street, waiting for the cars to stop. Behind her was the Dom Soyuza, its green paint shining where the early morning frost had melted in the autumn sun. She took the underpass beneath Gorky Street, and walked through to Gersena Ulitsa. Half an hour later she had let herself into the apartment in the small street off Pushinskaya Place.

She put the key on the plain wooden table and stood there looking around. It was an old-fashioned apartment, everything painted brown. But the furniture was good solid stuff, and comfortable looking. In the bedroom the old gas fittings had been left on the wall, and she guessed that they now housed the microphones and lenses that would record her life for the next few weeks.

Krasin had given her KGB coupons that she could spend at the Beryozka shops, and she had already bought some clothes. She took them from the paper bags with their pretty silver birch trade-marks and sat on the bed with the skirts and the sweaters, the two dresses and the coupons, spread over the coverlet. She also had Vneshtorgbank coupons she could use for buying food. She had counted all the coupons half a dozen times before Krasin had called on her. He seemed entirely indifferent to her now, the complete professional giving her her instructions.

The little social circus would be attending the reception given by the Foreign Ministry that evening for the two Nobel Prize winners announced the week before. Gromyko would be there, and so would His Excellency. Madame had a bug and was confined to her bed.

It was eight o'clock when the car had dropped Krasin and the girl at the gate by the Borovitsky Tower. They had strolled across the courtyard by the Armoury, and through the small gate in the wrought-iron railings. The lights blazed from the Grand Kremlin Palace and soldiers were opening the doors of the diplomats' vehicles and their drivers were being directed to the main car park.

The reception was in the great St George's Hall, and Krasin and Yelena walked slowly up the sweeping staircase to the first floor where the crowds of guests converged on the reception line. Inside the hall the six famous gilt chandeliers had been switched on, and down the long central table were photographs of the prize-winners and the research station in Uralsk where their work had been completed. The awards had been a welcome balm to Soviet agriculture after the Lysenko disaster, and the Swedish Embassy was being given the full treatment. The new hybrid wheat for cold climates was going to be called Svenska Nobel 193 to mark the award.

Yelena had seen the Ambassador at the centre of a group of Canadians and he had waved a hand to her and Krasin.

It was almost an hour later when he had spoken to her briefly. She had seen him, casually but intently, searching the faces of the groups of guests, looking for her as he stood by the mirrored doors to the Vladimir Hall. She had been able to tell him of her new address and had given him her telephone number. She had left a few minutes later and Krasin had driven her back to her apartment.

His Excellency had left after half an hour.

CHAPTER THREE

He stood at the top of the small flight of steps, his finger
just touching the white porcelain door-bell. Then his hand
came down slowly, and he turned towards the street. There
was still a fair flow of traffic and the car tyres swished on
the wet road. A group of youngsters walked by and shouted
something as they saw him. A giant jet was crossing the
city with its lights signalling to Sheremetyevo, and after it
had passed a tug on the river sent out its mournful sound.
The breeze ruffled his hair and he felt soft rain on his face.
It was like Glasgow on Sunday night when the crowds had
gone. But it wasn't Glasgow, it was Moscow. And somewhere in the red-bricked building the girl was waiting for
him. If he pressed that white door-bell it was going to make
a difference to a lot of lives. At this moment he was not
committed. He had done nothing more than talk to her,
apart from giving her a few trinkets. His desire must have
been obvious to her, just as her acceptance of it was
obvious to him. But they had never talked of lust or love,
not even affection. Neither of them had asked for anything,
but something had been given nevertheless. Something in-
tangible, and he wished he knew what it was. If he pressed
that bell he knew he would have her, and if he did, she
would have him too. He looked up at the dark blue sky
and then sighed just once as he turned and pressed the white
door-bell.

He stood inside the room, his coat-collar still turned up
up and his hands thrust deep in his pockets. As he leaned
back against the heavy door he looked at the girl as she
stood smiling with her hands on her hips. The thick blonde
hair hung in coils at her shoulders and the bare bulb cast
a flat, open light across her face. But it couldn't hide her

beauty. And even as he looked at her he knew that it wasn't beauty. Lydia and Adèle were beautiful. This girl was pretty, or maybe the word was lovely. The kind of beauty that upper-class snobs described as 'shop-girl pretty'. The big blue eyes were calm, the pert nose was as polished as marble, and her mouth was full and faintly defiant. She was wearing a charcoal-coloured dress and the one white button at her throat seemed to emphasize the scooped-out vent that showed the valley of her breasts.

As he stood there looking at her there was something he wanted to say, but it was as if there was some small gear wheel missing in his brain, like a telephone that kept ringing that nobody answered. Then she put out her graceful arms, and her hands waited outstretched for his. But his arms had gone around her and his mouth was on hers. For a moment his lust was all that was there, and then he pulled away, his hands clenched at his side.

'I came to talk, Yelena.'

She put her hand gently on his mouth and with her other hand she unbuttoned his coat. His face still serious, he laid his coat across the table and a button at the collar set the glasses on the tray clinking and ringing.

'Sit down, Jamie. Just sit down.'

And she poured two whiskies and handed him one as he sat awkwardly in the wicker chair. She leaned with one arm along the high back of the leather armchair, and she sipped from her glass and then rested that too on the chair. She looked across at the neat slim man with the tidy freckled face. The nose was too big and too long and the mouth was too small, but the slightly bulging brown eyes dominated the parts into a handsome whole. There were smile creases round the mouth, but not round the eyes, the left-over clues from a hundred diplomatic smiles that never included his eyes. His long fingers twirled the glass as he looked back at her.

'We don't need to pretend, do we, Jamie?'

He nodded but he didn't speak.

'So can I speak first?'

47

He half-smiled and made a slight bow of his head. 'Of course.'

'I like my times with you, Jamie, and I think you like being with me.' And now he was looking at her intently. 'And apart from liking me I think you want me. When a man wants a girl in that way he can make mistakes. Mistakes about liking, mistakes about feelings, and things can be said that are regretted when that need has been satisfied. You agree?'

He shook his head. 'Not in this case. Maybe a young man, but not me.'

She smiled at him fondly. 'No, Jamie, the older the man the greater the chance of mistakes.'

'Maybe.'

'So will you love me first before we talk?'

There was no need for him to answer, and as he watched, a slim arm went behind her and he heard the slur of a zip unfastening and the top of the dress slid down her arms and the skirt avalanched to her feet, and she was naked.

She turned to face him, and there was no pretence because she knew all too well what was wanted. Her big firm breasts quivered as she moved and her long legs were astride. And naked, she looked even younger than before.

The old-fashioned bedstead had been painted white and she had pushed the pillows away from her head. And as his hand had enjoyed her body she had looked up into his face and seen the excitement give way to tenderness, and then flare into lust. It had been almost an hour before his body had covered hers and now he lay between her long legs, his face against hers, a long swatch of blonde hair in his hand. When he moved to lie beside her she looked at his face and it seemed younger not older. And he spoke gently as her hand touched his cheek.

'So now we can talk, Yelena.'

She shook her head, smiling.

'Why not?' And there was a touch of indignation in his voice.

'Not while your hand is there.'

'Listen to what I have to say.'

She smiled back at him and nodded.

'I'm going back to London in five weeks' time. I want to see you every day that is possible until then.'

She smiled. 'Are you asking me or telling me?'

'I'm asking.'

She put her hand gently on his shoulder. 'Of course you can see me every day. You can come here whenever you can get away.' She sat up and swung her legs over the side of the bed and then she walked through to the living-room. She came back with the whisky bottle and the two glasses.

When she had poured the drinks she lay back on the bed alongside him. He lifted his glass towards her. 'Slainte.'

'What does that mean?'

'It's the same as "na zdrovie". It's Gaelic.'

She said 'Slainte' and slugged back the whisky in one mouthful. As his hand closed over one of her big breasts he looked at the pretty face. The gentian blue eyes were heavy-lidded and as his fingers squeezed and lifted the firm flesh she sighed and lay back, her head on the pillows, and the corn-coloured hair shone like metal. She watched his eyes go from her breasts to her flat, young belly, and then lower. As he looked, she opened her long legs and felt his body stir against her thigh as he looked at the mound between her legs. His fingers gently stroked the blonde bush that emphasized rather than concealed her sex. Her soft mouth was eager for his, and they kissed avidly as his hand moved on her with mounting excitement.

It was raining hard as he left the red-brick building and the embassy car was waiting for him at the corner of Tverskoi Boulevard.

Some days the Ambassador's official duties had made it impossible for them to meet, but they were the few exceptions.

For three weeks they had spent an hour or two together most days, either at the girl's apartment or at her mother's place in the country. Krasin worked hard to arrange official functions where the girl could be discreetly included.

When they were alone Hoult seemed relaxed and happy, and when they met at official occasions his diplomatic training made it possible for him to appear only friendly and courteous towards the girl. But the girl had no such training.

It was at a reception at the Embassy that the first signs of trouble arose. The Ambassador was entertaining his Foreign Secretary, accompanied by the Minister for the Arts; and the theatre, films, and the media generally had outnumbered the normal posse of Red Army and bureaucrats.

A new star at the Bolshoi was singing some of Rachmaninov's songs. She was half-way through the gentle song 'The Lilacs' when there was a crash of breaking glass and a girl's voice was shouting 'Komitet Gosudartsvennoy Bezopasnosti – shavki.' The singer hesitated then stopped, the accompanist trailed on for a few more bars and then stopped as a group of people were seen struggling with a pretty girl who was obviously drunk. The Ambassador walked over to the group. He feared that it would be Yelena, and as he approached he saw that he was right. She was wearing a black velvet evening dress that clung to her body and the long blonde hair was dishevelled as Krasin and another man tried to hold her and calm her. He pushed a man aside and he saw the tears on her face and the glaze in the wide blue eyes. She was screaming with her head held back and he put his hand on her shoulder. 'Yelenka, Yelenka.' He spoke softly and the girl's head came forward. She was quiet but trembling, as an animal trembles, and the red poppy mouth tried to smile. She said softly, 'Jamie, dear Jamie,' as she slid to the floor. Krasin had stooped and picked her up, and the silent crowd had made way for him as the Ambassador went back to his party.

It was almost midnight, and Their Excellencies sat drinking a last brandy with the Ministers and their wives. The Foreign Secretary was stretched out comfortably in the deep armchair, his tie undone and his shoes half off. He turned to Hoult and looked at him for a moment.

'What was up with the girl who made the disturbance, Jamie?'

'Too much to drink.'

'Well, you seemed to work your magic as usual, my boy. Ever the diplomat. What was she shouting about?'

'She said something nasty about the KGB.'

'Did she by God. What did she say exactly?'

'She said they were *shavki* – the dogs who sniff around garbage heaps.'

'Any idea why she was so het up?'

'Too much pressure. Too much drink.'

'Ah, that's the thing these days – pressure. It gets us all. I was telling the PM. I've not had two days off since we took office. Not two days in two and a half years. Hello! Here's that actor fellow.'

A servant was leading Krasin across. He was white-faced and barely under control. As he stood at the edge of the circle of chairs, Hoult waved him to an empty seat.

'Sit down, Krasin. Have a drink.'

'I came to apologize officially, Your Excellency. We bitterly regret the disturbance.' He turned to the Foreign Secretary.

'Sir Edward, it was especially regrettable that it should happen during your visit.'

'No need for an apology, dear fellow. We all have these little events to try us. Sit down and have a drink.'

As Krasin sipped a whisky he glanced at the Ambassador and saw the blue eyes looking back at him. There was no friendliness there, and he could see the barely hidden tension that showed from his mouth to his clenched fists. The Minister lifted his glass. 'What is it you chaps say, "Ra zdrovie"?' And Krasin responded quickly. There were more fences to be rebuilt here than he cared to contemplate. The operation was obviously over and now it was merely an effort to neutralize the situation.

'What happens to the girl? I understand you don't send them to Siberia any more.'

Krasin laughed. 'No, Minister. It's only engineers and technicians who go there nowadays and they earn four times what they'd get in Moscow.'

'We've been asking for permission for months for some of our chaps to visit your hydro-electric scheme out there. But we've had no joy so far.'

'Maybe I can speak to our people and see what can be done.'

'Good fellow ... Well, we must be off to bed. Got an early start tomorrow.'

And Hoult had strolled off with his visitors. Adèle Hoult sat on in the silence with Krasin.

'Is she your girl, Viktor?'

'We're friends, nothing more.'

'What do you call her?'

'Yelena.'

'Is Yelenka the same?'

'Oh, that's just a diminutive. Yelena means Helen in English and Yelenka is a form of endearment – little Helen – I guess it's like you say Nell – like Nell Gwynne.'

'And what will happen to her?'

'God knows. Forget it.'

'She looked very upset.'

'You saw her?'

'Yes, I was talking to your friend from Moscow Arts Theatre. I was just a few feet away.'

Their eyes met and held for long silent moments and there was anxiety and fear in both pairs of brown eyes. Finally she shivered and stood up.

'I shall be glad now when we've gone back.'

'Don't say that, Adèle. We've tried to make it fun for you.'

She smiled. 'You have, Viktor. I won't forget, ever.'

She opened her mouth to speak, hesitated, and then leaned forward and kissed his cheek, her white-gloved hands on his shoulders. They walked to the door and she stopped and looked up at his face.

'I've got a funny feeling about us, Viktor.'

'Tell me.'

'I can't. It's too vague. I think we're both frightened to-night.'

'Frightened about what?'

She sighed. 'I don't know. I don't feel secure any more.'

The guards smacked the butts of their rifles in salute as Krasin turned from his car and walked slowly up the wide stone steps. At the top he paused and looked back across the square. There were six inches of snow, and a bright full moon; the reflection of the moonlight had whitened the façade of the KGB headquarters. There was no traffic in the square but there were lights in the HQ windows, and he could feel a current of warm air from the big doors behind him. There were two messages at the check-in desk. He looked at his watch. It was almost two-thirty, but the tensions of the evening had pumped enough adrenalin into his bloodstream so that his tiredness had not taken over.

The others were already there and in addition he recognized Chebrikov from the Politburo. There was silence as he hung up his coat and walked over to the table. Soloviev waved him to a chair. He was barely seated before Soloviev started.

'Have you found out what caused the girl's outburst, Krasin?'

'No. She's unconscious still.'

'Where is she?'

'In the Lubyanka.'

'What explanation have you got for this shambles?'

'I said at the start that she drank and that she was difficult to control and ...'

Soloviev crashed down his hand on the table.

'— your mother, Krasin, you were there to control the situation.'

Krasin looked across the table at Soloviev, and the

others were silent. 'Comrade colonel, you are missing the point.'

He could have gone on to establish his argument but he deliberately refrained. If Soloviev wanted to play it tough then so would he. Soloviev had bubbles of saliva on his lips as his anger overflowed.

'Perhaps you can let us peasants into your intellectual secrets, Krasin.'

And Krasin noticed the slight retreat. Soloviev was backing into his colleagues for moral support. The turkey-cock face was red with anger, but the eyes were wary.

'The girl actually cares about Hoult, comrade. She is overwrought at what she is doing to him ...'

'Don't give us that crap, my friend. She's a twenty-year-old girl and you are supposed to be controlling her ...'

This time it was Krasin who banged on the table and his voice was loud and angry.

'Are you interested in the operation, Soloviev, or do you want to play the bureaucrat?'

The man from the Politburo put his hand on Soloviev's sleeve before he could speak. He nodded to Krasin and spoke very quietly.

'Tell us, comrade, what you wish to do.'

Krasin leaned back in his chair, his face drawn and pale.

'We can defuse the operation and let Hoult off the hook, or we can use the evidence we have already. Otherwise the original operation is over.'

'What was the Embassy reaction tonight?'

'Cool. Very cool. The Foreign Secretary accepted the apology and dismissed it as an incident, but Hoult looked at me as if he could kill me. His wife is already suspicious.'

'And what do you think Hoult will do now?'

'I've no doubt what he'll do. He'll freeze up. He won't go near the girl from now on. That little scenario will be enough for him.'

'And which course of action do you recommend, Krasin?'

'We go on. We face him with the evidence and blame the

girl's outburst on his relationship with her. Then we do as we intended, smooth it over, let him off the hook, leave him alone, and hope that he appreciates what we've done for him.'

'And what will we have done for him?'

'Saved trouble with his wife, saved a political scandal, saved his career.'

'What do the rest of you feel?' The Politburo man looked at the others.

Kuznetsov couldn't disguise his contempt for Krasin. 'I think Krasin has spent too much time with foreigners. I vote we should forget the whole thing and hold an enquiry into Krasin's handling of the operation. He would be better confining his talents to the theatre.'

The Politburo man made no comment and his face was impassive as he nodded in turn at the others. There were no takers for a decision. He turned back to Krasin.

'When do you suggest we tackle Hoult?'

'When the girl is dried out. We put her before the district court. I'll tip off the foreign press and she can indicate that some man is the cause without naming names. We then approach Hoult as if she has told us what has been going on. The magistrate suspends the trial in mid-evidence and if Hoult reacts our way we stop the case and shuffle the girl out of Moscow.'

Kuznetsov half turned and his grin emphasized his thin mouth.

'So you can get back to screwing the girl yourself, eh Krasin? Is that what you want?'

Soloviev's big hand clamped over Krasin's arm as it swung across the table.

'You go too far, Kuznetsov. Comrade Krasin was fighting Germans while you were learning your alphabet.' He leaned forward and looked at Krasin.

'We'll decide tomorrow, Krasin. Get some sleep.'

James Hoult had returned to his office after seeing his guests to their rooms. He switched on his radio and turned it to the BBC. There was nothing at all on Radio 4, there was a test carrier-wave on Radio 3 and on Radio 1 some juvenile moron who'd got a hit in the top twenty was giving his views on sex, religion and abortion. He switched off with anger. There was no consolation there, no bench-mark to compare a way of life. He walked across to the corner cupboard and took out a triangular Dimple Haig. He poured himself a drink and sat down at his desk.

What kind of man was he? He would have said a puritan. Not a Scottish puritan, but a natural puritan. And yet. It was Adèle who had once said it. She had been listening to a gramophone record when he came into the room. He had stood there listening, and when it was over he could hardly speak, and there had been tears in his eyes. When he had asked what it was, she had noticed the crack in his voice and she had looked at him with surprise. 'Jamie dear, I wonder about you sometimes. Inside that cool exterior there's a romantic bottled up. Some day it's going to get out and then we'd all better watch out.'

She had smiled at him. 'Anyway it was Mendelssohn, his Violin Concerto.'

He shook his head in an effort to dismiss the thoughts. The girl was surely in some Moscow cell and he couldn't bear to think of her alone and unhappy, deserted and ill. He had had his route carefully planned out but that was hopeless now. Maybe nearer the mark was that he wasn't a puritan, or a romantic, but a peasant with a good disguise.

The Russians were puritans, they would be at home in Edinburgh and Cardiff. They were peasants too, whatever they pretended. He reached inside for his wallet and took out a small, square photograph. It was cracked down the centre but that pretty face was there, with the blonde hair heaped up on top like a Greek goddess, and the big soft eyes squinting into the sun, and the wide, soft, mobile mouth caught in mid-smile. And he wanted her. Wanted those heavy breasts in his hands. And the long tapering legs as she lay on the bed, smiling as he looked at her body and the amused, loving, smile as she opened her legs to show him the excitement of her sex. He had never believed that love and lust went hand in hand but he knew that this was very close to that. The youthful erotic body aroused him as he had never been aroused before, it wasn't just its beauty, but her open pleasure in his excitement. The soft mouth, the big breasts, the exciting sex, were offered generously like fruit and flowers. And his need was not just to have her but to be with her. But even away from the overwhelming sex there was the same concern to please him. She touched his face, his hands, with her slim fingers, and she gave him her thoughts and her feelings without reserve or caution. Despite their different roles they were much alike really. No intellect, but peasant wisdom and animal pleasures.

He knew what he *should* do but he also knew what he *would* do. This mental exercise before he did it was only to get back the breath to do it.

There was notepaper and envelopes in the rosewood escritoire, and he took out a small sheet and wrote a few words. He pressed the button on his desk and then folded the sheet and put it in an envelope. The red sealing-wax was spitting and flaring as the messenger came in and stood waiting. His hand reached out for the official embassy seal, hesitated, and then withdrew. Turning over the envelope he wrote a name with a slight flourish. As he turned it to the blotter he looked up at the messenger.

'Ah, Burton. Give this to the chauffeur and tell him to deliver it immediately.'

It was four o'clock in the morning and still snowing.

CHAPTER FOUR

Krasin had fallen into the disturbed sleep of exhaustion and he heard the door-bell ringing before he recognized what it was. He switched on the light, put on his blue track-suit and walked slowly down the concrete stairs.

He recognized the embassy car and the Russian chauffeur, a KGB junior lieutenant. It was too dark in the hall-way to read the note and he went down the steps and stood with snow over his ankles as he held the sheet of paper to the reflected light. It was very brief, on official embassy notepaper. It just said,

> Krasin,
>   I want to see Andropov
> immediately. I suggest 8 a.m. at
> Dzerzhinsky Square.
>   Hoult.

Krasin looked at the chauffeur. 'What did he look like when he gave you this?'

'I didn't see the Ambassador, the messenger gave it to me.'

'Did they ask for an answer?'

'No.'

Back in his apartment Krasin looked at his watch. It was 4.25. He reached for the phone.

Yuri Vladimirovich Andropov pushed aside the breakfast things and reached for the files again. He remembered the matter being discussed at a Collegium meeting eight months ago. He had not seen any great chance of success. The KGB had tried out this sort of exercise some years back on the French Ambassador. The practicalities had worked well enough but there had been no pay-off. Junior embassy staff were just as useful, and much more vulnerable. Ambassadors didn't get their postings to Moscow by being naïve. They had too much to lose to play around. But he could see why they had all been tempted in this case. Britain was an important Soviet target, and the chance of pro-Soviet pressure right at the top was worth a lot of effort. He pushed the files aside and walked over to the window. The snow was quite deep outside on Kutuzovsky Prospekt but the sky was clear and the sun was shining.

It was a long time since he had first started work as a telegraph operator and he had made no real progress until he became a Komsomol organizer in 1936. His group of partisans behind the German lines had not only been successful but the experience had taught him how to analyse men's characters and motives. He had been an ambassador himself and he knew all too well the pressures. He had been the Soviet Ambassador in Budapest during the 1956 uprising and he had had to use those old partisan skills in luring Nagy and Malater to their deaths, so that the compliant Kadar could be installed in their place. There were some who said that ambassadors these days were no more than messenger boys, but he knew that the Presidium had based its actions in Budapest on his own assessment of the situation. The British Prime Minister would be making decisions that would sometimes be based on Hoult's analysis of Soviet intentions. A friend that deep in court could be invaluable.

He turned to the red telephone and called Malygin. He told him to contact the Ambassador through Krasin. They *would* meet at 8 a.m.

As the new chairman of the KGB, Andropov had created new tensions. Work norms had been tightened but privileges had been extended and as his car pulled up at Dzerzhinsky Square he saw that although it was well before eight o'clock the six pedestrian gates to KGB headquarters already carried a flow of staff. They didn't start officially until nine, but by arriving early they could have cheap, good breakfasts at the restaurants in the basement and on the eighth floor.

The main steps had been swept and he walked up carefully, nodding to the guards as they presented arms. His bodyguard was watching the traffic in the square until Andropov was in the lift to his third-floor office.

On the huge desk the Kremlevka telephone was blinking. He picked up the receiver and stood with his coat half off as he listened. The Kremlin wanted an updated report on 'illegals' in the United States and a member of the Presidium was querying the figures in a KGB study on Turkish aircraft spares. When he had put down the receiver he dictated a note on to the permanently active tape-recorder. Then he told the operator that there would be no more calls until he had dealt with the British Ambassador.

There was a knock at the door and Krasin came in with Hoult. Andropov noticed that they both looked drawn and tense. He wondered what Her Brittanic Majesty's Ambassador had to say to the head of the KGB.

He listened carefully as Krasin made the introductions. Then he walked from behind his desk, his hand outstretched.

Hoult was surprised at Andropov's appearance. He was a tall, academic-looking man, his English was near perfect and his smile amiable.

'Good morning, Your Excellency. Let us sit down more comfortably over here.' And he waved his arm to the embroidered antique chairs. Krasin stood while the two settled themselves. Andropov ignored him as he beamed across at Hoult.

'I wonder whether we could release friend Krasin? Or would you prefer him to stay?'

'I think we should talk alone.' Andropov noted the chill in the voice and he nodded to Krasin to go as he offered a cigarette to the Ambassador. Hoult shook his head and sat straight and upright in his chair. Andropov was aware of the deep breath that Hoult took before he spoke. Another sign of tension.

'Comrade Andropov, can I suggest that we omit the formalities and talk quite frankly?'

Andropov nodded and smiled, and shrugged like any Frenchman.

'But of course, Sir James, of course. I'm an old-fashioned man. I like the courtesies but I like to get down to the heart of things as quickly as possible. Now what can I do for you?'

'For at least six months your organization has spent a lot of time, a lot of money, and a lot of energy trying to contrive a situation that would allow you to put pressure on me.'

Hoult paused momentarily for a denial, but Andropov was silent. The look on his face was of patience and understanding, but completely non-committal. Like a hotel manager waiting to hear what the guest's actual complaint would turn out to be.

Hoult continued, 'I can compliment them for their energy but not for their subtlety. Somebody had decided that it was your young ladies who would produce results. I have no idea why Lydia Ouspenskaya was suddenly withdrawn but that is of no importance. Even before she left I had got to know another of your young ladies – Yelena Markova. I assumed that she was something to do with your organization because she was always around with Krasin and his little circus. The difference was that *I* chose her, not Krasin. It was obvious to me that at some stage this was recognized, and that, maybe, is why Lydia Ouspenskaya was removed.

'I also assumed that your organization was, as usual, collecting evidence of my meetings with these girls. Photographs, films, the usual blackmail material. And I equally took it for granted that before I left for London, or maybe after my return there. I should be confronted with this material so that I could be pressured into some sort of co-operation with your people. I too am an old-fashioned man, and because there would be no element of surprise I should

61

have told your people to go to hell.' He stopped as Andropov leaned forward.

'Sir James. We are both men of the world, both experienced in the ways security organizations work and I should think that it is possible that what you have just told me is substantially true. I could not admit that officially, even if, after checking, I found it to *be* true. But I cannot believe that you came here solely to tell me that my young men have been naïve and clumsy.' The big brown eyes were still gentle, and the smile, although amused, was still friendly.

'Comrade chairman, you will already know that there was an incident yesterday evening at my Embassy. Yelena Markova was drunk and caused a disturbance. Krasin took her away. I suspect that she will be punished because she has spoiled your operation. I ask that she shall be released immediately and that she should be allowed to go to London when I return there.'

There was a long silence and Andropov's eyes were on Hoult's drawn face.

'Tell me, Sir James, before I answer you. What do you feel about the Soviet Union?'

'If you disbanded the KGB it could be a good country to live in.'

Andropov smiled slowly. 'At least two members of the Politburo would echo your sentiments, except that they would prefer execution to disbanding. Now, let us get down to this problem.' He raised a hand as he saw Hoult about to speak.

'A moment, Sir James. Let me say right away that whatever you wish will be arranged. We have been impressed with your record here in Moscow. All we ask, all we expect, from Western diplomats is neutrality. We don't ask for approval or admiration, we accept hostility, and we are grateful for impartiality. All *I* ask is that I am in your confidence. What happens when this young lady is in London?'

'You mean that this will be arranged?'

Andropov smiled. 'But of course. You look, Sir James, like a man who had worked out a threat and finds it was

62

not needed.' He leaned over and patted the Ambassador's knee. 'Tell me about this girl. I do not know her. I understand she is very pretty.'

'Yes, she is pretty but ...' Andropov had put up his hand again.

'Sir James, you were going to call me comrade chairman again. It it not necessary. I like you and we shall be good friends. My name is Yuri, and I shall call you James. There is no need to tell me more. I have had over thirty years looking at men, trying to guess how they will react in certain circumstances. There are still things to learn, but I shall not learn them. I am too old a dog to start again. I know enough about you from our meeting this morning to ask no more. Just one thing worries me though. You know what it is?'

'I'm afraid not.'

'I think it was that Irishman of yours, Oscar Wilde, who said it best. He said, "Why does he hate me, I never did him a good turn." Something like that. So will you hate us because I have helped you?'

'Can I be rude in the face of your good will?'

Andropov grinned and spread his hands. 'But of course, my friend. Tell me.'

'In any other country but this I would not need to ask your help. We could do as we wished.'

Andropov's face was stony for only a second and then he laughed. 'That's not quite true, of course, and you know it. But I take your point. Anyway that answers my problem. Now to practicalities. I will arrange for the young lady to be released if she has been detained, and I will instruct Krasin to arrange a suite for her at one of the central hotels. I assume that you can arrange her visa and so on in London. If she wants to work at our Trade Mission there, that too can be arranged.'

He held out his hand, and clasping Hoult's firmly he said, 'Feel free to ask me to make any arrangements you wish. Maybe we shall meet again before you leave, but if not I hope you have every success in your new post. Try and remember us kindly.'

Before the Revolution the building had been the main offices of the All-Russian Insurance Company. Now it was the Lubyanka, the KGB's own private prison.

Hoult had gone in with Krasin and as they walked down the gloomy concrete corridors Hoult was revolted by the contrast between Krasin the theatrical charmer, and the man who walked beside him, at home in these grim surroundings. The girl was sitting on a wooden bed, her head in her hands. She was still wearing the black velvet dress. It was torn and stained with vomit, and as she looked up at Krasin, Hoult saw the swelling at the side of her face and the bruises on her slender neck where they spread across her shoulder. Her hair was unkempt and her eyes were dull. Then she saw Hoult, and he saw the lovely throat flex as she swallowed. She tried to stand as she whispered, 'Jamie, oh Jamie, they've got you too,' and she had slumped back on to the wooden boards, unconscious and inert.

Hoult turned to Krasin and his anger shredded his voice. 'I gather you'll be the messenger boy, Krasin. Don't come near her, nor me, nor the Embassy. Phone if you have anything to say to me.'

'Sir James, believe me . . .'

Hoult's face was red with his feelings and he swung round aggressively towards Krasin. 'Stop playing games, Krasin. It's over as far as you are concerned. Just get her a car, I want her to go to the National.'

It wasn't Krasin's day. The whole team had been assembled in Andropov's office. Nobody had been invited to sit, and Andropov himself had let his anger spew over them all, but it was Krasin who took the brunt of the abuse.

Andropov was a cultured man but he hadn't been appointed chairman of the KGB for his culture. He was standing at the side of the farthest window and between each bout of invective he looked from the window across the square as if it fed anew the flames of his rage. His hand trembled with passion as he pointed at Krasin.

'All the while he *knew*, Krasin. Right from the start. You must have looked like country bumpkins, poncing around with your fancy people. And what do we get out of it – he screws the arses off a couple of swallows and then wants to take one back to England. And *you*, Soloviev. Was there no psychologist's report on this man before you started? Mother of God, I have to sit here listening to his crap while I look like some pimp fixing him up with a girl. All we needed was a bloody gypsy violinist playing "Ochi chornya" and it would have been complete.'

He paused for breath, but only for seconds. His voice was softer now but full of menace. 'But I tell you all *this*: from now on you report direct to me. You do everything exactly as I say. Not one word, not one action different from my orders. Because that little bastard took me for a a ride this morning. You cretins left me no choice. Any pressure on him and the whole thing would have exploded, so I end up like a country inn-keeper, fixing for the tax inspector to screw the kitchen-maid.

'Krasin, you will do whatever he asks, but you keep me informed. Every hour if necessary. Soloviev, you will arrange that Hoult will be invited to all the important functions until he leaves. He must believe it all worked this morning. All will be sunshine and flowers. Understand?'

And he'd waved his hands at them to go away, as if he were shooing out a flock of pigeons. When they had gone he pressed the internal phone for Malygin.

'Malygin. Check for me who we've got in London who's *really* bright. Not too old because it's a long-term operation. If there's nobody really good already there, make me two recommendations for new appointments.'

CHAPTER FIVE

Hoult was awake, lying on his back. Yelena's smooth leg lay across his body and her arm across his chest. The curtains were open on the big windows and he could see the thick cottonwool snow piled on the window ledges. From time to time he could hear the faint beat of an orchestra that came from one of the lower floors of the hotel. And in the far distance he heard the wail of a train siren. The sad, lonely note matched the tumult in his mind, and its overtones echoed in the strange room, matching his feeling of being in limbo. The sad wail was vaguely reminiscent of the senseless pop songs that so annoyed him. They had words that matched that wail. Self-pitying and self-important – 'by the time I get to Tulsa – or Phoenix – or somewhere'. The lonely words of disorientated people, and now he found they matched his mood. Maybe he was an elderly drop-out. But that could be a very slippery path and he refused to explore it.

Adèle had gone back to prepare the house for their return in two weeks' time. So now he slept each night with Yelena, and he had never known such pleasure. The seeming casualness that made no demands on him, required no pretences, social or otherwise. The open pleasure that she found in just being with him had unlocked his reserve. It was as if some caged and wary animal were released into its natural environment. And her delight that her body excited him, her instant awareness that some way of standing or lying, some line of her legs, some movement of her breasts aroused him. He had never seen himself as sexually restrained but he knew now that he had been. The gestures to propriety, the restraints required of respect and gratitude, the conventions of sexuality, the bad manners of looking and touching had made it all mere formula, a tribute to fair ladies with no vulgarities. And now in his fifties he was let loose in this sexual toy-shop with a girl who was so young and pretty that it was like some sexual fantasy. And she loved him.

Even without the sex, he was, for the first time in his life, loved and admired for just being himself. Not as the gallant Black Watch major, not as the just administrator of enemy territory, not as a shrewd banker, and certainly not as a diplomat. But in the times like this when he was awake on his own, it seemed like madness, incredible, and dreamlike. He fell into a troubled sleep wondering what to do about Adèle, wondering where he belonged, wondering who the hell he was. As his eyes closed he worked out how he'd get her an Irish passport and a background to match. Once she was out of the Soviet Union she'd be safe.

Andropov had called in Krasin and Soloviev, and they now sat in the big embroidered armchairs that smelt faintly of mothballs. Alongside Andropov was a middle-aged man, dark-skinned with high cheek-bones, and his hair crew-cut. His dark blue suit was well cut and his shoes were foreign-made and elegant. A gold-rimmed monocle hung on a thin braid from his collar.

When they had settled, Andropov introduced the stranger.

'Professor Simonov spent some years at Leningrad. He has made a special study of West European psychiatric conditions related to interrogation under pressure. Am I describing your work correctly, Professor?'

The man had shifted briskly in his seat and looked at the others. 'My initial work was the study of returned prisoners of war, their psychological reaction to the stresses they had undergone, and their assimilation into normal civilian life.

'I was then asked to establish a training routine for the KGB and GRU, to enable their operatives to resist interrogation by the enemy. From this, my department moved on to examine methods of improving our own inter-

67

rogation methods of hostile agents. This, of course, included considerable research on the reactions of Americans and West Europeans to all types of stress.'

He nodded briskly towards Andropov who looked round the half circle and said, 'I have asked Professor Simonov to give us an analysis of the British Ambassador.'

He waved and nodded to Simonov who reached down for a clip-board at the side of his chair.

'I must emphasize, gentlemen, that this is no more than a general comment to assist your consideration of how to control this situation. I have seen your films, listened to your tapes and read carefully your written reports. Chairman Andropov has also given me some background.

'Additionally I have seen the photocopies of the medical records of this man. They were of no significance. Clinically he has no problems, he is a very fit man.

'I have also to emphasize that most of my work has concerned Americans, and although you already know that there is a vast difference between the Russian and the American temperament and attitude to life, there are still further differences between the Americans and the British. My experience with the British is very, very limited. This man is in fact a Scot, and that makes my material second-source all the way through.

'However,' he smiled, 'he is a man, and that is the basis on which we start.

'This man came from a quite humble background, indifferent educational record and then he achieves success as an active soldier. He was for almost six years in the services. And that is our first point to remember. But let us continue. From this progress he becomes an administrator in occupied Germany. We can surmise that it was his marriage to the daughter of an influential man that got him his banking work. He had by then considerable international experience, particularly in Europe, but many will have had equal experience who did not become bankers. Finally, as an old friend of the Prime Minister, he comes to Moscow as Ambassador.

'We know from his war record that he is physically brave. We have some experience that he has moral courage. He is involved with politics but he doesn't join a party. He gave pro-French advice as a banker that must have been unpopular to his associates. All the assessments of him that we have been able to obtain show him as a man who not only fitted easily into new environments, but as a man who was also successful in many different fields.

'And now what do we have? This rigid conformist in his early fifties seems to have gone wild, like some undergraduate sowing his wild oats.' He looked around for disagreement and finding none he continued. 'Now this is my assessment.

'The six years in the services were from about his nineteenth birthday. A time when most young men are being irresponsible, particularly Europeans. I have seen American and British studies on this that were examining the wave of divorces and promiscuity that hit those countries about ten years after the end of the war. Their conclusions were that the thirty-year-olds were reverting to teenage behaviour. Living that part of their lives that allows them irresponsibility but which the war had deprived them of. Lack of stability, avoiding family responsibilities, the start of the drug wave, that sort of thing. But this man was still caught up in the official web, still part of the machinery of authority. And now, long afterwards, in a strange country, away from those restraints, nature is catching up on him. He too is subconsciously claiming back those years.

'I believe too that his career has been thrust on him. He has gone from one sphere to another but through force of circumstances not design. He may not value his success in the way that other men would.

'Apart from all this, he is the normal confused "homo sapiens" that he appears to be.'

He looked at Andropov, who turned to the others. 'Any comments or questions?'

It was Soloviev who spoke. 'How would Professor Simonov suggest we use his analysis?'

Simonov looked for permission from Andropov, and when he nodded, he leaned forward.

'If you apply open pressure on this man he will tell you to go to hell. He would be prepared to lose everything except this girl. Let him simmer. Help him where you can. Slowly, slowly this man is going to destroy himself. His wife will probably leave him, and if you have the means you should precipitate that. His circle of friends will gradually disappear. He has the strength to cope with this, but he will be very vulnerable. Gradually more unsure of himself in his private life. Compensating in his political life by even greater efforts. He will need bolstering, and you can do this. Not only with our own people, but with the other Europeans. He should be made to look like a man of influence in Europe rather than just the Soviets. That's the line I should take.'

'How far do you think we can use him?' It was Soloviev again.

Simonov leaned back and smoothed his trouser leg as he thought. He looked up slowly and faced Soloviev.

'You can use him two ways, but if you want to use both you'd have to go very carefully. He will be amenable to pushing our point of view because you can convince him carefully and gradually, and he will be receptive. You can use him in practical terms if you prepare the ground slowly.'

'You mean as an agent?'

'Yes, I mean as an agent.'

CHAPTER SIX

Aware that Adèle was looking for a home that they would never use, Hoult knew that he had to tell her. He wasn't the kind of man who could happily accommodate a wife and a mistress. He had never condemned those who could. Why tear up the lives of wife and children when all you wanted was the new excitement between some young girl's legs? But the possibility never entered Hoult's thoughts. It wasn't his style, and it wasn't what he wanted. But he knew that he was facing a situation that would do him damage. For almost the first time in his life he was going to do what *he* wanted, ignoring obligations, convenience and expedience.

Three days after his meeting with Andropov he had contacted Andropov's office for a further meeting. An hour later he had received a formal and printed invitation to a reception that evening at the Foreign Ministry, in honour of the departing Soviet gymnasts who were touring in South America. A telephone call from Krasin had established that Andropov would be at the party and a private meeting had been arranged.

Just before ten o'clock he had been invited to have an informal drink in a private room. Andropov was there, talking to another man who was introduced as Soloviev.

Andropov had been all charm and had waved him to a leather chair alongside an open fire. Andropov had stood, drink in hand, his back to the fire like any English squire. He waved his glass towards Soloviev as he looked down at Hoult.

'I've asked comrade Soloviev to join us because there are things he can do to make things easier. Documents, formalities and so on.'

'That's what I wanted to talk about. The documents for the girl – Miss Markova.'

'Of course.'

'I should appreciate your help in getting her a passport.'

'No problem there, James. It can be available at an hour's notice.'

'I want her to have a United States passport.'

Soloviev had looked quickly towards Andropov who ignored him. He half-closed his eyes as he drew on his cigarette. Then he turned, put his glass on the mantelpiece and turned back to look at Hoult.

'Can we be absolutely frank with one another?'

'Certainly.'

'Wouldn't it be easier for you if the girl was on the strength of our trade mission? I understand it is very near the main part of London – Highfields, Highlands, some name like that.'

'Highgate.'

'That's it. I'm afraid I don't know London at all.'

'Perhaps I haven't made the position clear. I'm going to marry her.'

Andropov reached behind him for his glass, and Soloviev admired the casualness of the defence gesture. But Andropov was already speaking again.

'Is this going to affect your new appointment, do you think?'

'Not if she is an American.'

Andropov looked directly at Soloviev. 'You wanted to say something?'

'A suggestion, Minister.' And he turned to look at Hoult. 'I can see your point, Your Excellency, but there are people who might have seen the girl in Moscow, who would recognize her. Very unlikely, because she is not well known in foreign circles, but a possibility. I would suggest that she should be American-Polish. Even people who might have seen her here would not be sure of her nationality. It could explain a lot.'

Hoult nodded. 'I agree. That would be much better. Could it be arranged?'

Andropov intervened. 'Yes, of course. It will take a little

72

longer. You realize that. When it involves an official ceremony like marriage we should want the documents to be virtually the real thing. What would be involved, Soloviev?'

'Passport, birth certificate, revenue document, visa, and health certificate. She would have to go there – to the United States. A week somewhere, New York or maybe Pittsburgh. Could take two weeks. That would be better.'

'How would she travel there?'

Soloviev looked at Andropov who nodded.

'Moscow to Dublin. Dublin to Montreal. And then we'll see her over the border to a place we've got in Albany.'

'D'you want me to help with the English visa?'

Soloviev half-smiled and opened his mouth to speak, but Andropov put up his hand to stop him.

'I think it's best if we look after all the arrangements, James.' He poured himself another drink. 'Where is she now – still at the National?'

'Yes.'

Andropov nodded to Soloviev. 'All right, comrade. We'll leave it all to you.'

Soloviev had shaken hands and left. Andropov sat down opposite Hoult. And leaning back comfortably he said, 'Have you told your wife yet?'

'No. I shall fly to London in a few days and tell her then.'

Andropov looked at the Ambassador through half-closed eyes.

'Have you told the Prime Minister?'

'I shall tell him while I'm in London.'

'What do you think his reaction will be?'

'Surprise, he'll be sorry for both of us.'

'Not shocked?'

Hoult had smiled. 'He's been married three times himself. I think he knows the score about private lives being private.'

'Ah, yes. I'd forgotten that.'

He had not forgotten but he was relieved that Hoult seemed to have considered all the angles.

* * *

73

A Foreign Office car had taken him up to town from Heathrow and he'd booked in at the Reform Club. He hadn't told Adèle exactly when he would be arriving. She was at the cottage at Lamberhurst and he would call her tomorrow and go down and get it over.

They'd got the Christmas decorations up at Charing Cross Station as he went through the gate for platform 5. The sun was out as the train left Sevenoaks but the orchards looked wet and stark to match his mood. He took a taxi from the station at Tunbridge Wells and the house looked empty as the car turned into the drive.

Adèle had been out when he phoned, and he had left a message with the housekeeper. And it was Mrs Hoskins who answered the door. Adèle was still shopping in the village. Already he felt a stranger in the house. He wandered through the rooms, but there was nothing that invited him; he wanted to be gone. He searched through his mind for past Christmases but there was nothing there. They belonged to another life, somebody else's life.

He had been sitting on the big double bed in their bedroom when Adèle had opened the door. She still had on her coat and a fur hat, and her face was rosy from walking in the cold. He stood up as she came across to kiss him and she sat in the big chintzy chair. The brown eyes were soft and she rested her chin on her hand as she looked at him.

'I've been waiting for you, Jamie.'

He looked back at her, surprised. 'How d'you mean?'

She sighed. 'Waiting for you to tell me what's to happen to us.'

'You knew?'

She shook her head slowly. 'No, Jamie, I didn't know. But I'm a woman and I knew things were wrong, and I guessed the rest. And I knew that when you were ready you'd tell me. It's the girl, the one at the reception – Yelena, isn't it?'

'Yes. I want to marry her.'

74

'Have you spoken to Travers yet?'

'No. I haven't spoken to anyone but you.'

'Will it stop the new appointment?'

'Why should it?'

'The fact that she's Russian.'

'I'm not going to tell them.'

'That's not like you, Jamie.'

He half smiled. 'You'll be the only one who knows my guilty secret.'

'And the divorce. How do we go about that?'

'Travers can do all that.'

'And there's nothing I can do to change your mind?'

He shook his head, but said nothing.

'You may not believe me, Jamie, but I hope you'll be happy in your new life. I've been thinking so much about us, and you, in these last few weeks while I was on my own here. And I realized for the first time how much I should miss you. I tried to work out what I could have done differently so that it never happened. I didn't get the answer, and now it's too late.'

She looked across at him as he sat, hands in pockets on the edge of the bed, and she realized that he looked somehow younger. He could be listening to comments from an older sister.

'What are you going to do, Adèle?'

'I shall go back to Paris.'

'I'm sorry about all this.'

'You don't have to say that, Jamie. I know you'll be sorry that I'm unhappy but I do understand about you. Not properly, but at the back of my mind I understand.'

'I don't deserve such understanding.'

She stood up. 'Shall I tell the boys?'

'Thank you.'

'Will you stay for a meal or a drink?'

He wanted to match her mood, her conciliation, but he couldn't.

'I'll ring for a taxi.'

'No. I'll take you in the mini.'

At the station she had taken his hand and kissed his cheek.

'I'm not going to be the traditional wife, Jamie, who tears up her husband because it didn't work out. Think of me when you're happy, and that I've tried to help. And I'll think of you.'

'When will you think of me?'

She put her head back against the car seat and closed her eyes.

'When I hear a Scots accent, when I see soldiers, when it's night – and when I hear Mendelssohn's Violin Concerto.'

He had bent over and kissed her and then he was gone.

The interview with the Prime Minister had been as he expected. There had been surprise and much sympathy, and then the subject had been changed to the PM's forthcoming trip to Moscow. There had been a hint of the House of Lords, but all in good time.

Moscow was in the grip of winter and Yelena was already in New York. He took eight days to hand over to the new man. The Russians had gone out of their way to pay their respects and his farewell reception had been at the Polish Embassy. The Poles were arranging a party in New York the day he arrived there. And this, ostensibly, was where he would first meet Yelena.

He had flown direct from Moscow and there had been a four-hour delay at Goose Bay and the fog had only cleared long enough for take-off before it came down again over the desolate airfield. But Hoult was happy in anticipation of seeing the girl again.

Washington had booked him in at the Waldorf and the Polish invitation was waiting for him at reception. His host was the Permanent Representative at the United Nations of the Polish Government, and he begged Sir James's presence at a reception in honour of the Mazowsze dancers.

A car had called for him just after eight and a few minutes later he was going up in the lift in the UN building. He had seen Yelena straight away and she saw him too. But it was nearly twenty minutes later when he was introduced to Miss Helen Markova. They had left separately at ten o'clock, had met again at the main entrance, and walked up East Avenue. They stopped, the wind pulling at their clothes, and there was a special delight in embracing in public. Even a public that that was more intent on holding on to its hat.

They had spent a week together, at theatres and concerts, and the columnists had not let it go unremarked.

The British visa had been easily arranged and there were two or three photographers as they walked through to reception at Heathrow. There had been a paragraph or two in the next day's papers, but that was all.

PART TWO

CHAPTER SEVEN

There was that stink of wet coats in the cloakroom. Faintly reminiscent of the army but not typical of the cloakroom at the Reform Club. There had been one of those short, sharp, April showers at 12.45 and only the tycoons without coats, but with chauffeur-driven cars, had escaped.

By 3.30 most of the coats had gone. Hoult and his guest were washing at the big bowls and half a fat cigar was smouldering on the mirror shelf. As he dried his hands, Lord Tutin had reached for the butt and had held it in his teeth as he struggled into his jacket.

'I've got a car waiting if you want a lift, Jamie.'

'Thanks, but no. Anyway I've got a phone call to make before I leave.'

Tutin reached for an umbrella and turned back to his host.

'I'll be reporting to the board tomorrow and I'm sure you'll be getting a call from Toby. We couldn't have done this deal without your help. We've had a chap sitting in Prague for seven months and they wouldn't even see him. IBM, CDC, Univac, they've all had a pitch but we couldn't even get that far. This order is the biggest we've ever had anywhere, and it'll open the door for a lot more from that neck of the woods. We shall make it known that it was your advice that did it.'

Hoult had taken his arm and strolled with him to the door. Tutin stood for a moment as if reluctant to go. Then he said, 'I was sorry to hear the news about you and Adèle. These things do happen these days. Take care of yourself, my boy.' And he had stepped carefully down the steps to the waiting car.

James Hoult walked slowly up the stairs and ordered another coffee. There had been plenty of similar comments when the divorce had gone through, but that was three months ago. The little piece before the wedding in *Private Eye* about him seeking his consolation with the young blonde had now given rise to another little flurry of condolence. They never mentioned *Private Eye* but he guessed that that was the reason.

It was nearly five when he went down to the cloakroom. His coat was dry now and his hand went deep into the right-hand pocket. The small packet had gone all right, and he wondered idly who, in the Reform Club, they had used to pick it up.

He stood looking at the ticker while they called him a taxi. The dock strike was entering its seventh week and the hijacked plane at Heathrow was still there. The Government would not agree to freeing the four Irishmen who had blown up St George's Hospital. Negotiations were continuing. The price of gold had fallen 8 points due to a release of Soviet gold into Zurich and Cairo. The PM was meeting the striking North Sea oilmen later that day. The Minister had denied that petrol rationing was being considered. Congress was considering the US participation in NATO, and a schoolgirl in Wiltshire had given birth to quads.

Hoult had never been a man to make friends, and when the word got around that the marriage had broken up because of his dislike of the social whirl there were few who found it all that surprising. Hoult's appointment was not an official one but as part of the Prime Minister's personal staff. The Press gave him the normal grace period during and immediately after the divorce and because he worked in the background and never sought publicity they gradually forgot him.

Oddly enough he and Yelena went frequently to concerts, the theatre and the ballet. More often than he had willingly gone in the old days. And what was more, he enjoyed and looked forward to these outings with Yelena. They seldom entertained, and when they did, their guests were generally from industry. Men who sought his advice on overseas trade with foreign governments. They attended no public functions and the invitations that were so politely refused in the early days gradually ceased to be extended. He kept up no contacts with the world of diplomats and that world was glad to see the back of him. He didn't belong. An experiment that hadn't worked out.

He left Downing Street just after eight and walked back in the mild spring evening to the flat in Ebury Street. Adèle had claimed no maintenance from him and he was reasonably well off. He still had the house at Lamberhurst but he had put it to the agents in Tunbridge Wells. He had never felt loyalties or attachments to houses, and since the divorce the village seemed to have drawn away. The gardener had decided to retire, and the housekeeper had given notice. Nobody in the village had been even unpleasant, but it had withdrawn from him and he was conscious of the faint disapproval. Yelena had been down with him for one weekend. Nobody had called, and even the man who brought down the red dispatch boxes had seemed conscious of the atmosphere as he sat in the kitchen alone.

They had been married six months now. It had been a quiet Thursday ceremony at the Chelsea register office. A Scottish MP had been best man, and the PM's private secretary had been Yelena's support. They had all lunched at Scott's and an official car had taken the couple to Heathrow for their flight to Edinburgh. He had taken her to see the house in Methil where he was born and a few people who had recognized him had given them a nod and a diffident smile.

There was a call for him as he turned the key in the door, and he kissed Yelena as he took over the receiver. It was the PM's secretary, who wanted to read out the draft of Hoult's recommendations to the PM about the Soviet Trade Loan. His report had recommended a tactful refusal, and the grounds he had given were sound and well reasoned.

He had deleted what he felt on reflection was a repetitious argument, and had told her to type it and put it to the PM as soon as possible. It was to be discussed at the next day's Cabinet.

Although they had had the routine meeting only three days previously, Andropov had seen the London report and had called a special meeting.

He had been very smooth before the meeting started, but Soloviev had too much experience of the man not to pick up his controlled irritation. He was not surprised at the attack that came as soon as they were round the table.

'You've seen what's happened, Soloviev? He's closed down on us, says our demands are too many. I warned you about this *months* ago. I've looked at your current requests. The NATO report. North Sea oil figures. The United States threat to pull out of the UN. And half a dozen piddling things in addition. He's been co-operating with other ministries here as well. And now he's called it off.' He paused for breath, but not for the others' comments, and he went on. 'The whole subversion programme in Britain is ready to go, and here we have a man whose advice will be taken at every turn, *against* us, instead of *for* us. Admittedly he's picked and chosen what help he has given us in the past, but by God we've never had a man so well placed to help us before. And now at best he's neutral, and at worst against us.'

Andropov leaned back in his chair, his hands still on the table. He looked first at Soloviev.

'Well, Soloviev, what do we do?'

Soloviev had lasted too long in the jungle of the KGB to get landed with that sort of responsibility but he knew Andropov well enough to know that he would want some sort of response.

'What were the reasons that he gave?'

'Just what the report says – our demands are too many.'

'Any indications of other reasons that he hasn't told us?'

'Such as?'

'Are they checking on him at all – the British security people?'

Andropov reached for a small pad and made a brief note. Then he nodded at Soloviev.

'I'll check on that. Anything else?'

'Any problems with the girl?'

Andropov shook his head slowly 'No, we've had regular reports on that area. They seem to get on all right.'

'What exactly do we want him to do on the subversion operation?'

Andropov looked round the table and nodded at the others without including Soloviev. 'That's all, comrades.'

When the others had gone, Andropov lit a cigarette and made himself comfortable, one hand shunting the gold lighter backwards and forwards along the edge of the pad.

'Our people over there have done a first-class job. In two years they've got the Press and radio hamstrung with new laws. They can't print a thing if our people don't approve. We give them rope – but not where it matters.

'We can tie up all transport any time we want – the railways, the docks, the lot.'

'Is that the unions?'

Andropov smiled and shook his head. 'We stopped bothering with them in '74. We don't need them, we've got our own people controlling their workers. Anyway, to continue. They haven't pulled out of their slump and there's real friction now between management and labour, and labour and the middle classes. But the middle classes are waking up fast. They've suddenly realized what's been happening. If they're given time – say six months – they could put the clock back for us by ten years or more.

'There's a group of influential people from both the major parties putting pressure on the Prime Minister to resign and let the people decide at an election. Our information is that the Opposition would win hands down. They would revoke the laws that suit our people and there would be a reactionary dictatorship for years.

85

'If we can bolster up the Prime Minister for a minimum of one month, but better still two, it would be too late for these people. Hoult is the man who could do this. Maybe not even he could do it, but if not him, then nobody. And that would mean years of planning, years of effort, wasted.'

Soloviev had decided what to say long before Andropov finished speaking. He left a reasonable interval for apparent consideration of the chairman's statement.

'It may sound crazy but I think we should use Krasin.'

Andropov's head jerked up, his eyes half-closed in surprise.

'You're right, colonel. It does sound crazy. It was Krasin who screwed up the original operation.'

'I don't agree, comrade chairman. The first girl and the husband were a million to one chance. Nobody could cover every tiny outside chance. And the second time we were all glad of a scapegoat. He *had* spoken about the girl's drinking habits. Maybe it wasn't an actual warning, but he *had* put it on the record. And one way or another it worked. We have used Hoult to good purpose. It's only at this stage that he's become a problem.'

Andropov stubbed out his cigarette, carefully and slowly, and without looking up he said, 'Soloviev, you should have been a bloody lawyer. It's a good argument nevertheless, but I think Krasin was a scapegoat for Hoult as well as us. Any other reasons for suggesting this?'

'Last New Year and the previous one, Hoult sent good wishes to the Prime Minister. Officially, through their Embassy. And privately he sent his good wishes to Krasin. Also Krasin has been the one who has kept an eye on the girl's mother.'

'Are they close, the girl and her mother?'

'I'd say no. I don't think they give a damn for one another. It's a bit of a farce but we've gone along with it.'

'Have we got any theatre people going to London in the next few days?'

'I don't know, comrade chairman.'

Andropov stood up and walked over to his desk, and

dialled and sat down. When he had talked he sat there for a moment before he came back to Soloviev. As he bent to sit down he shook his head. 'Nothing at all.'

'We can put something together in twenty-four hours.'

Andropov pursed his lips for a moment. 'Right, you do that, Soloviev. See me tonight. Here. At seven.'

They sat round the table long after the meal was over, Hoult and Yelena, Toby and Lucy Marr, and the PM's private secretary. It had been Toby Marr who had led them on to Soviet affairs.

'I gather they're going to put on a special "do" at the Ministry after the Czechs sign the contract. Are you going to bring the lovely Helen?'

'When is it?'

'Day after tomorrow. Tuesday.' He turned to the PM's secretary. 'Any chance of the PM coming, Tim? Give it the Good Housekeeping Seal of Approval.'

'What time is it?'

'Well as long as they don't sod about at the last minute I'd say about three. So's we catch the news at six.'

Tim Hart had been a journalist before he was taken on by the PM, and industrialists always assumed that his heart was still in Fleet Street. He went along with the charade because it was easier than saying that he wanted a knighthood.

'Depends how long it lasts. He's got a Question Time at three but I could probably sneak him out for fifteen minutes about four.'

Lucy Marr was renowned for her acid comments, so they were not surprised when she sniffed and said, 'It really has come to something when we need to get the Czechs to fill our begging bowls. Do we need to celebrate that?'

Her husband was used to her outbursts and he beamed at her affectionately. 'That order is going to keep a lot of people in jobs, my girl. And that includes me.'

But she was not to be assuaged so easily. 'Is that all that matters? Do we *have* to play along with tyrants for our daily bread?'

'You afraid it may be catching, Lucy?' Tim Hart was smiling as he lifted his glass to the irate lady.

'My God, if it's catching we caught it long ago. This country's like a prison camp. Editors have to get some Minister's permission to print what the unions don't like. They made us sell our little place in the Algarve. For foreign exchange they said. To plug up the escape hatches more like. We've had strike after strike this year. As soon as one lot is settled the next one starts.'

Her husband nudged her gently. 'You can't blame the unions for that, sweetie. They're generally unofficial.'

'What the hell does it matter what they are, they're bankrupting us all.'

Hoult had tried to turn the conversation, but she wouldn't have it. She waved an elegant hand at him. 'Don't be the diplomat, Jamie. There's been too much of that. It's becoming an offence even to criticize these days.' As Tim Hart chuckled she turned on him fiercely. 'It's not a joke, Tim. Your damn people have killed private medicine just to please the yobs who wash the bed linen, but it hasn't improved the Health Service. Far from it. You can wait a year now for an operation. It's just like bloody Russia.'

Hoult sat wiping his mouth with his napkin, and now he laid it down untidily as he leaned forward. 'I only wish it *were*, Lucy. There are more doctors in the Soviet Union than we have here.'

'For God's sake they've got more citizens.'

'No, I mean *pro rata*. They've got a doctor for every 400 people. We've only got one for every 900.'

The woman looked nonplussed. 'I thought you were anti-communist, Jamie? I've heard you criticize them often enough.'

'I'm not anti or pro, Lucy. I just like facts, that's all.'

She shrugged her shoulders defensively. 'So if it's all that good why do they need to censor Solzhenitsyn?'

Hoult smiled. 'For the same reason the Labour Government censored the Crossman *Diaries* a few years back. It's just part of governing a country.'

For a moment she hesitated. Then she smiled and touched her husband's hand as she looked across at Hoult.

'You still haven't told us if Helen will be at Toby's bun-fight?'

Hoult raised his eyebrows in query to Yelena, who smiled and nodded.

But Hoult and Yelena were not at the signing ceremony and its aftermath of celebration. Late on the Sunday evening he had been called to Chequers. There had been criticisms of internal British policy at one of the United Nations sub-committees. Twenty Opposition MPs and a sprinkling of lawyers had submitted a dossier which the sub-committee were passing to the Committee on Human Rights for their consideration. The dossier recorded a long list of alleged breaches of the UN pledges on freedom. A sub-section was being passed to the International Court of Justice claiming breaches of the Constitution, one-party government, and discrimination in employment, coupled with government pressures on the judiciary and the media.

Although a public threat had been made previously by the signatories, that a dossier would be submitted to the UN, the PM had seen it as no more than a threat. The British representatives at the UN had seen the documents and had immediately phoned the PM with a précis. The Prime Minister was livid, and when Hoult arrived he had been closeted with the Law Officers.

The instructions had been very explicit. He was to fly immediately to New York and make a formal protest to the Secretary-General. If the American media latched on to it, he was to give a press conference, and if he could imply that the signatories were a bunch of fascists, so much the better. There was no doubt that the PM was rattled. He had even mooted the idea of libel actions and injunctions, but the Attorney General had tactfully headed him off into more dignified channels.

The official car had taken them from Kennedy to the Waldorf. Hoult sat on the double bed reading the long list of names from the thick reference book. Yelena was taking a shower.

When she came in Hoult had looked at her body as she towelled herself dry. It still had its magic for him, especially when he could watch her, intent on something, unaware that she was observed. She was twenty-three now, but if anything she looked younger than when he had first seen her. He had noticed her even before the Lydia episode. It was even before he had realized that Krasin was playing games. She had been one of a party at the Stanislavsky Music Theatre. They had had two boxes and Yelena had sat in the front row of his box. She had leaned with her elbows on the red velvet of the surround, her little finger curled back between her teeth, and she had gasped and smiled her reaction to the dancing, while the others maintained a more dignified enthusiasm. The big breasts had strained against the white wool sweater and he had been surprised at her slim waist and long legs when she had stood drinking champagne later at the Embassy.

He pointed at the open pages of the thick book. 'Have a look at that list, Yelenka. See if you recognize the names.'

She sat back on the bed and plumped up the pillows for her back. As she wriggled to make herself comfortable she saw him looking at her body. She put the book on the bed beside her and, smiling, she opened her legs. 'You want to dry me there, Jamie?'

He laughed. 'Read that damned list.'

'What is it?'

'It's the list of all the Soviet staff at the UN.'

She went down the list, her finger moving slowly. Finally she looked up and shrugged her shoulders.

'Two names I know, but I've never met them. Maybe I better stay here. How long shall we be in New York?'

'Two days, three at the most.'

There had been soothing noises from the sub-committee.

It was no longer their hot potato, and they could afford to appear accommodating. The secretariat had been very cool and formal.

He was standing at the main doors waiting for the official car when he saw Krasin. He was with another man and they had walked past him up the steps. He had half-turned, and Krasin had turned too, leaving his companion and walking back down the steps. For a moment they both hesitated and then they were shaking hands.

'Jamie. What are you doing here?'

'Making protests, as usual.'

'And how is – how is your wife?'

'Very well indeed.'

'How long are you here for?'

'A couple of days, not long.'

'Could we meet, d'you think?'

'Would that be wise?'

'Maybe not. I'll be in London on Thursday for a week, could we meet there?'

'I should think so. Phone me at Downing Street. Your Embassy will have the number.'

Krasin looked at him with the big brown eyes. 'I was very sorry about that shambles in Moscow, Jamie. It was my fault entirely.'

'These things happen. Best forgotten.'

And he'd waved and walked down to the Rolls.

CHAPTER EIGHT

The uniformed porter came round from behind his desk in the lobby and then stopped, smiled, and touched his cap. 'Ah, it's you, Mr Kenny. I didn't recognize you for a moment.'

The big man laughed. 'I've come straight from the office.'

The porter moved over to the elevator and pressed the button for the seventeenth floor. As they waited he said, 'They're all up there already.'

Hank Kenny had slipped him a five-dollar note and the elevator gates had closed behind him.

It was against all the CIA rules, but poker addicts are a law unto themselves, and the fortnightly poker game was only passed in times of major crisis, like war, or a brand new chick who hadn't been house-trained yet.

The others were already at the table. Sweaters, jeans and sneakers, and a pall of smoke, and country and western on the hi-fi. There were jibes at the dark blue suit and a fresh pack of beer came out of the triple Westinghouse. They checked the times on their watches. No matter how long a game of poker lasted, to its devotees it was always too short. The house-rule was that they finished on the stroke of three, no matter what.

All four of them were senior operatives for the CIA and the school had been going for nearly two years. They had vague ideas of what each was up to in working hours but there was no probing in business areas. From time to time there was some mild cross-referencing, but no more than could have been done officially if it had been necessary. Good friends they might be, but when they sat down for poker that went by the board. One thing they all agreed on. Poker is a game for blood.

Hank Kenny had spent three hours one evening analysing the playing foibles of his friends, and although it was generally Lew Malins who took home most of the pot, the loot was fairly evenly spread, and that's how it should be. With poker you played with your peers. If you played with 'softies' you could get classed as a hustler, and if you went above your league you'd surely get skinned.

Lew Malins never talked while he played, and he never looked pleased or sorry, whatever the state of the game. And even his mother would never get to see his hole card without putting in the last bet to call his hand. As far as Hank Kenny could tell, Lew Malins bet his good hands up, and he never stayed in for the hell of it. He may bluff from time to time but nobody had ever caught him at it.

Steve Kowalski was a poker fidget. He 'read' faces and watched fingers for signs of despair or elation, and two or three times in every session Kenny had seen him raise a 25 cent pot by two dollars and look pleased when he gathered in the loot. Kenny reckoned that risking two dollars for 25 cents wouldn't ever make you a poker player. And Kowalski had never worked out one of the facts of life. Good poker players call you twenty-four times to one.

Con Hallows was the Boston Irishman, built like a house and ugly with it. But ugly or not, Con Hallows laid more chicks than the rest of them put together. It was the crinkly-eyed smile that did it. Con Hallows played to the book. He bet on the value of the first two cards and if the hole card was less than a ten spot he folded, unless he was holding a pair. When he stayed in, and somebody's second upcard gave him a better picture, Con Hallows backed down. He never raised on a weak hand. He never won much, and he contributed quite a bundle to Lew Malins.

As always, at midnight they broke for sandwiches and coffee. It was Lew Malins who had started the gossip. 'Any of you guys seen the report on the British at the UN?'

Hallows had sprayed salami in his eagerness. 'Their guy was at the glass box today. Making a formal protest.'

'You see him there?'

'No, it was on TV. Interview at the Waldorf, and then a

shot of him talking to their guy in the VIP room at the UN.'

Malins had nodded. 'You see that gal with him. His wife, I guess. Pretty as a picture and was *she* stacked. Only a girl, and he's got grey hair.'

Steve Kowalski grinned. 'Maybe you'll get one like that, Lew, when you've got grey hair.'

Malins stood holding his beer and his tongue was sorting out his teeth. 'I saw a piece in the *Times* said she was one of your lot. Polish-American.'

Kowalski waved his sandwich. 'Who isn't, buddy, who isn't?'

Malins' head swung round. 'You reckon the Brits are going to get their arses kicked, Hank?'

'Not so it hurts.'

'So why they send this lord over?'

'He's not a lord, he's a knight.'

'OK. Knight then. Why the hustle?'

Kenny had looked down at his beer and when he looked up his voice was dry and quiet.

'You interested officially, Lew, or you just trying to find a lead to the little gal?'

'You trading, pal?'

'Sure.'

'OK. I phone you tomorrow. First light.'

Krasin had telephoned the man at the advertising agency at eight. He had gone through the elaborate routine of calling, then hanging up and repeating the routine four times. The man's voice at the other end had said, 'Things go better with Coca-Cola,' and Krasin said, 'I've made contact', and hung up.

The word was passed back to Moscow by short-wave radio inside the hour. Andropov had been at the All-Russia Chess Finals when they gave him the message.

Hoult had been back in London three hours before he had had a chance to make contact. He had walked from the flat in Ebury Street to Victoria Station. He looked at the graffiti in the third telephone kiosk. And there among the plaudits for Arsenal and Queen's Park Rangers he saw it. 'Young model 01-087-4840.' He reversed the last seven digits and waited.

'01-048-4780. Can I help you?'

'I was contacted in New York. Is it official?'

'Yes, that is quite all right. Good night.'

He replaced the receiver, and then, under some foolish compulsion, he dialled the graffiti number. After only one ring a girl's voice said, 'She's very beautiful, dear. Five for the full treatment and we're in Warwick Road near the . . .' and he hung up, depressed beyond contemplation.

The Prime Minister was in one of his Stanley Baldwin moods. Man of the people looking across the decades was the general theme, and it had served him well a hundred times with constituency parties, cronies and the media. Only the blandishments of Tim Hart had stopped him from being photographed at the weekend leaning over a fence looking speculatively at the handful of Large Whites that wallowed and grunted in one of the out-buildings at Chequers. But the three men who faced him across the Cabinet table now were not going along with the script.

He had asked what he referred to as the 'ring-leaders' of the newly formed British Action Group to meet him at Downing Street to discuss their *démarche* at the United Nations. He had got out of the habit of dealing with probing journalists and politicians. The media, whether it was the newspapers or the BBC, knew that if they tried the old probing question gambit the interview would be terminated instantly. And they knew too that next time they wanted the licence money increased or they had a strike on their hands they would be on their own, with a few of the PM's cronies looking solemn and talking about 'alternative management structures'.

But these people were not cronies. Certainly they were politicians, but all three of them were almost completely immune to any of the pressures he was used to applying.

One was an international lawyer, and the other two had incomes based on overseas investments. Maybe Hart should encourage a few press pieces on the scandal of citizens who kept their money overseas.

As the spokesman outlined their points, he looked at them without blinking. These little physical things could be very important in creating an image of unflinching determination. When he held up his soft hand to interrupt, his voice was quiet with reasonableness.

'But Mr Price-Waters, let us put aside the detail for the moment. Have you *really* considered the damage you are doing to the country in the eyes of the world?'

'The damage has already been done, Prime Minister. And it has been done by your Government. We no longer have a free Press – they're controlled by the Minister of Labour Relations. We no longer have a choice in medicine or education. You've handed us all over to the Marxists, Mr Prime Minister, and we are going to stop you.'

The Prime Minister hesitated for a moment. His instinct was to close the meeting immediately but these men had the air of men who could succeed. He had made his political reputation by leading, and holding together, a party that ranged from the far left to the evangelical, and surely his mixture could be made to work on these men too. He smiled his knowing smile, the one he used at ragged Cabinets. The one that said, 'We all know what it's all about, let's work out a deal.'

'But what you're saying is, that Parliament has decided certain things. They are now the law, but we'd like to change the law. And that is democracy. Parliament, the House, is the place for your efforts to be made, not the United Nations.'

'Prime Minister, your party had a small parliamentary majority, but it has a minority of votes cast at the last three elections, and you have steam-rollered through extremist Bills that are wrecking the country, dividing it from top to bottom.'

'This sounds like the Reds under the bed scaremongering all over again.'

'They are not under the bed any longer. They're *in* the bed and it's time we called a halt.'

The Prime Minister looked at his watch. 'Gentlemen, we must meet again soon, but I have another appointment.' And as they left he smiled because he knew how to tackle the problem now. He'd have a Royal Commission. That would smother them for a year. He would do one of his TV specials to announce it. He cast a few opening sentences as he sat in the car on its way to Paddington. 'There are some amongst us' – no, better – 'There are *elements* amongst us.' And maybe 'amongst us' sounded too cosy, perhaps just 'there are elements who'. By the time he was on the train there were other things to occupy his mind.

CHAPTER NINE

The big boat swung slowly at her mooring alongside the small wooden jetty. There had been snow in the first week of April and although the sun was now so hot that there was condensation on the stanchions, the river was running high from Oxford to Penton Hook.

Across the teak table in the saloon two men faced one another with an open file in front of each of them. The big man was the current head of SIS, and he was big all over. Massive shoulders, big hands and a big head with a mass of wavy grey hair that looked as if it had been set by Vidal Sassoon himself. His mouth was open as he listened to his companion reading out the last paragraph of the typed report. When it was finished he closed his mouth and looked out of the windows. There was a pale grey-blue heron perched on the 'Danger' notice that faced the entrance to the lock on the far side of the Thames, and the cluster of ducks were paddling furiously against the current just to stay still. He looked back at his companion.

'Well the thing is, do we show it to the PM as it is?'

'What's the alternative?'

'We can tone it down, omit the rough stuff, or even tell him we need more time.'

'You think he'll throw it back at us as it is now.'

'No, that's not his way. But you've got to remember these people are his old cronies. They all started off together, and he can't believe that any of them could want to bring the country to a standstill. And what we have put here doesn't *prove* they have manoeuvred him for two years. You can see a clear pattern of subversion, a movement of *real* power away from Parliament to individuals and pressure groups. But you can't say they haven't used the legal processes to do it. He can say they were elected to carry out reforms and these *are* the reforms.'

'But the harm they have done is there to see. Millions of man-days lost in wild-cat strikes. The Press attacked even for mild comment. Mobs controlling the docks, mines, the generating stations, and virtually everything else that can bring the country grinding to a halt.'

'That's one interpretation, Jock, there are others. And maybe this is what he wants himself.'

'I don't believe that. Most of all he wants to stay in office. When he got back last time he had to give the left a lot of power to keep them under control. He thought they would stick to the rules. They didn't, and they were never under his control. Look at the times he's appealed to the grass-roots over their heads.'

'Remember what somebody once said, "Everybody hates inflation but they love what makes it happen." You tell the man in the street that we've got a quiet dictatorship and he'll laugh at you. He's got more money and more clout than he's ever had.'

'So what do we do?'

'We give it to him, just as it is. That's what we're here for.'

'And expect the chopper?'

The big man laughed and shook his head as he folded over the cover of the report.

'No, he won't do that. He needs us. But you just imagine what it's going to be like for him. If he doesn't go along with it, he knows his days are numbered; they're nearly ready to take over. If he agrees with it, he's going to start cutting them down to size, easing the power back to Whitehall and Westminster, and then they'll get him. His feet won't touch.'

'You think there's nothing he can do to stop it?'

The big man sighed. 'There's something he could do all right. He could instruct us to sort the buggers out.'

'How long would that take?'

'We could stop the rot in two weeks and clean them *all* up in six months. There are plenty of backbenchers he could promote. He'd have more friends than he's got now. Let's chug up to Temple and have lunch.'

Hank Kenny had done his trading with Lew Malins and two days later he was on the plane to London. He had walked out through the 'Nothing to declare' exit but he had been stopped for a spot-check.

He had two suits in plastic covers slung over his shoulder and a medium-sized canvas grip. The customs man laid them out on the platform and went through them carefully. He checked them and then looked up, pointing at the camera slung round Kenny's neck.

'What's the camera?'

'A Nikon F2S.'

'How much is it worth?'

'I paid just over five hundred dollars for it, a couple of months ago.'

'Where?'

'Cambridge Camera Exchange, Seventh Avenue, New York City.'

'You know that it's an offence to import goods into the UK?'

'Sure, but this is for my own use. I'll be taking it back with me.'

The customs man smiled. 'That's OK, sir,' and as Kenny moved off the man shouted, 'Have you got keys in your trouser pocket?'

'Yeah. Say, what is all this?'

'Give them to me and I'll hand them back the other side of the barrier, otherwise you'll set the alarm going.'

'Alarm?'

'Yes – it's anti-hijack routine.'

As Kenny took back his keys he wasn't so sure the Brits were as dumb as they seemed. But it was just as well they hadn't wanted to open the Nikon. He took a taxi to South Audley Street and then walked. The office had booked him in at the Europa, and as he buttoned up his shirt he looked across Grosvenor Square towards the Embassy. He'd be about as welcome there as snow in June.

Krasin had contacted Hoult through the PM's office and they had met in St James's Park. When Hoult had first been approached they had asked for his opinion on quite minor aspects of Anglo-Soviet relationships. But as the months went by he had been asked what were the views of others, the Cabinet, the Opposition and the PM himself. Although Hoult had not gone into great detail it had been enough to fill in a lot of the blanks in the KGB jig-saw. There had never been even the slightest hint that he might be under an obligation to them, and there had been no mention of any of the incidents in Moscow. It was discussion rather than informing. There were not even the routine politenesses of enquiries after his wife's health. Every effort was made to create an atmosphere where merely casual conversation was being conducted with a man of wide experience.

The first compromising act that he had performed was quite minor. His name was used as a reference for a girl who had applied for a post in the visa section of the Passport Office. She already had the recommendations of a civil servant and of her vicar.

When they had asked him for sight of a Cabinet document it had not concerned direct British security. It was the current Admiralty appreciation of the Turkish Navy. He had had some qualms when he passed them the Joint Staffs' feasibility study of Allied reaction to a Soviet takeover in Berlin, but it seemed an unlikely event in any case. The information on the Chinese he saw as of no significance. The correspondence between the US President and the PM had been a possible refusal, but when they told him, correctly, the gist of it, the precise words seemed a very small step forward.

The SIS study of current KGB operations in the UK had definitely been a sticking point, and that he had refused. Four days later Yelena had received a letter from her mother. It had been pushed through the letter-box during the night and bore no stamp or postmark. It appeared that it had been discovered that she was not entitled to her small pension because the Moscow records showed up the arrest of her daughter without indication of any court decision. It was all a mistake, she wrote, and they would soon sort it out. But Yelena had known better, and Hoult had known better too. Hoult had phoned the Soviet Ambassador and His Excellency gave his assurance that it would be rectified immediately.

From that point Hoult had been asked for material on very few occasions during the last three months. He had told his contact bluntly that he had had enough. His contact had been understanding and sympathetic, and Hoult had slid back into a feeling of security. They probably realized that he had amply repaid any obligation there might be.

Krasin had given him Moscow's gossip as they sat in the sun on the bench beneath one of the big beeches, and it was almost half an hour later that Krasin had put his hand gently on Hoult's shoulder as he turned towards him.

'Would you help me, Jamie? Me personally?'

'Depends what it is, Viktor.'

'We believe that your security people have made a report to the Prime Minister about the political situation. Our people think it could harm relations between our two countries. We very much need to know what is recommended in that report.'

'This is hardly personal, Krasin.'

'When the thing with Yelena and you went wrong, I was blamed for it. I have been out in the cold ever since then. They have given me this chance. They insisted that I ask you. I told them that I was probably the last person you would help.'

Hoult looked at Krasin's face. He looked much the same as he had looked a few years back, in Moscow, but away from his own setting the charm was rather spurious, a con-man's charm, charm that was after a pay-off.

'I think your friends in this country have gone too far, too quickly, Krasin.'

102

'Is that what the report says, Jamie?'

'More or less.'

'So what's going to happen?'

At that moment Hoult felt all the conflicts of his life focused on to this situation. For a moment of only half-caught comprehension he saw a hundred images, and felt a dozen emotions – love, ambition, indifference, and the boredom of a tolerance that flowed from indifference. Phoney or not, Krasin had talent, and if it had not been for Krasin he would never have met Yelena. And without Yelena there would have been nowhere to retreat to. They all saw the relationship as lust for a pretty young girl, and that had undoubtedly been the key that opened the door. None of them knew of the security that he had found beyond the door. No need to be a winner, none of the pathetic social whirl. To be Jamie Hoult was enough. His indifference, in the last year, to the outside world had given him an impartiality that had been admired and respected by men of importance. They saw it as wisdom, but he knew better. To see good in the Soviet efforts was not difficult. Good was there. There was good in this country too, but both countries had their share of hypocrisy and evil. The hypocrisies were the same, only the evils were different. What did it really matter which set of values prevailed? He could survive with either or neither. All he wanted was to be left alone with Yelena. Away from the ardent contrivers on both sides. No country, no beliefs, no dogma, mattered to him any more.

Hoult saw the genuine anxiety in Krasin's eyes and the late afternoon sun magnified the lines etched on the actor's face. This was the man he had heard reciting Shakespeare sonnets and Wordsworth, with genuine love. And this was the man who was at ease in the musty, damp corridors of the Lubyanka.

'The security people have put forward plans.'

'Tell me, Jamie. What will happen?'

'I haven't seen the written report.'

'Will you see it?'

103

'Probably.'

'Will you keep me informed?'

Hoult stood up and the sparrows fell back a few feet. He shook his head. 'That would be going too far, Viktor. You'll have to try your other friends.'

CHAPTER TEN

Even on a fine spring day Ackers Row in Pimlico would not have given pleasure to anyone other than a demolition contractor or a developer. The local authority had condemned it twelve years previously and twice a year the housing committee discussed its redevelopment. The verdict was always the same. The increased building costs estimated by the City of Westminster surveyor were noted, and it was agreed unanimously that the scheme would be postponed until the financial climate was more suitable.

Meanwhile a whole range of small businesses were allowed to occupy the hotch-potch of premises on three-month leases. Between the stench-ridden premises of a dealer in hides and skins and a manufacturer of car roof-racks was a pair of double doors that gave on to a sloping, cobbled runway that led to a glass-fronted office with the sign 'Layton Studios' stretching across the whole of its broad frontage.

Inside was a reception area with a display of indoor plants and a modern Bryant's water-garden. On the walls were model reference sheets and 20×16 blow-ups of advertising photographs. Beyond the reception area were two offices, a large, high-ceilinged studio and two darkrooms. Beyond the second darkroom, and reached through a metal door were several other rooms including two bedrooms and a large room furnished in black leather and pine.

The big man from SIS had waved the two Americans to the leather chairs, and bottles and glasses were ranged on the low, white, circular table. Whilst there was no official liaison these days between SIS and the American Embassy, there was a close unofficial working relationship that suited both parties, and saved both countries' taxpayers considerable amounts of money. There was a tacit agreement that when awkward facts were uncovered by either side about the other, there would be cross-referencing before the facts went higher up the line to either the head of SIS or the Director of the CIA.

The big man had raised his glass and smiled. 'OK Pete. Make the introductions.'

The short, thick-set American sat right on the edge of his chair. 'I've brought along Hank Kenny. He operates for us in New York. I'd have sent him on his own, but I felt I should explain that in this case the local ground rules don't apply. The Director of the CIA has already been informed, because the information turned up in New York, not in London. However it concerns London, and it concerns your people. Our instructions were that Kenny should be put in touch with you personally.'

The big man nodded. 'Your people gave us due notice.'

'So. Well I'll let Hank deal with this in his own way.'

Hank Kenny was formally dressed and that made him ill at ease. What he had to say made him even more so.

'Sir. I was about to enter the UN building some days ago. I was accompanied by another man, a Russian named Krasin. On the way in he saw a man who he obviously knew well. He left me for several minutes to talk with the man. I recognized the man as Sir James Hoult, who was at the UN on official British business.

'I also saw Sir James on newscasts. On one of these occasions he was accompanied by his wife. I recognized his wife. I am in doubt about her real identity, sir.'

The big man had recognized the clipped police-type report as being some sort of defence mechanism, and wondered why an identity problem caused so much formality.

'Maybe you could put me a little more in the picture, Mr Kenny. Do pour yourself another whisky, and please take my word for it that everything you tell me is absolutely confidential. There's no need for formality.'

'Sir. *Who's Who* and all the reference books list her as

106

previously being a Miss Helen Mackay. The newspaper clippings mention that she is American/Polish. But I first saw her in Moscow, where I was stationed for two years. I saw her on other occasions in the company of Krasin, the Russian who spoke to Sir James Hoult.'

'I gather you've done some checking of the records, Mr Kenny.'

'Yes, sir. I have. The birth certificate, the tax certificates and other documents used to obtain a passport were all forged documents. We have traced their source and have affidavits from the man concerned.'

'So what is the real name of the lady?'

'I don't know, sir. All I can say is that when I met her she was a Russian citizen.'

The big man scratched the side of his jaw, thinking.

'What was this man Krasin in Moscow?'

'He's a well-known actor. He broadcasts frequently. And he's a lieutenant-colonel in the KGB.'

'And have you done any checking in Moscow?'

'No, sir. I was specifically instructed to cease all further enquiries until you had been informed.'

'And what construction have you put on this information, Mr Kenny?'

Hank Kenny shot a glance of appeal at his companion, but there was no response. He and Lew Malins had spent hours kicking it around, but that wasn't an official evaluation. Hank Kenny decided to keep to the book.

'I've not been informed of any evaluation, sir.'

The big man took a deep breath and then stood up.

'You must have drawn certain conclusions or we shouldn't be here right now. Just tell me what *you* think. You don't have to be right.'

'Well, in my book people who use forged documents are criminals. I think they should be prosecuted.'

'That's what you think should be *done*, not what you think were the reasons for the deception.'

The big man swung round and looked at Kenny.

107

'Well, sir, putting the softer interpretation on the evidence, the girl has deceived her husband about her nationality.'

'Go on.'

'Or maybe she hasn't deceived her husband; maybe he knew and they both wanted to deceive other people.'

'Why?'

'Because maybe he would not be able to hold a confidential post if he were married to a Russian.'

'Mr Kenny. Hank. We had a Soviet ambassador in London who married an Englishwoman. It didn't harm his career. He became Soviet Foreign Minister.'

'It might have made a difference if his wife had previously been the mistress of an MI6 officer.'

'Have your people got a file on Krasin?'

'Yes.'

'Have you seen it yourself?'

'Yes, sir, I have.'

'And?'

'And there's a whole wad of evidence that he's been used by the KGB to cultivate foreign diplomats. Especially the British, the French and the Americans.'

'What was Krasin doing in New York?'

'He was having preliminary talks about a USA tour by the Leningrad Symphony Orchestra and several Soviet soloists.'

'And your role?'

Kenny managed a half-smile. 'I was detailed to help him.'

The big man turned to the second American. 'And what's the official Langley view, Pete?'

'We think you've got trouble. Real trouble.'

'Has the White House been told?'

'You betcha.'

'And?'

'That's why we're here, Matt. There's been nothing passed back here to Downing Street. That's your pigeon. But I have been ordered to co-operate with you in any way you

108

require – provided you treat the matter seriously.'

Matthew Layton didn't take kindly to having the buck passed to him when it had strings attached, but he knew that he would have done the same if the positions had been reversed. The only difference was that the Americans would have told *him* to go to hell. But they had gift-wrapped it all nicely by coming direct to him when they should have gone direct to DI5. This was a UK security problem and not part of SIS's amorphous patch. But for a year DI5 had looked a 'leaky' vessel, not to be relied on. The Americans would have heard the rumours, and there were even indications that they might have experienced the leaks first-hand.

Layton sat down, the big hands clasped, and his biceps straining the light-weight mohair of his suit. His brow was furrowed like corrugated cardboard and the piggy eyes were crinkled in concentration.

'I think for the moment, Pete, we will not tell Downing Street. Give me twenty-four hours to sniff around and we'll get together again here.'

'Krasin is in London now. Arrived this morning.'

'Oh, Christ. OK, can you meet me here this evening, say six o'clock? Same procedure as this morning.'

'OK, Matt.'

'Where can I contact you?'

'The Embassy, care of the Ambassador's secretary.'

Layton half-smiled. He already knew that Pete Maddox was dossed down in the CIA 'safe-house' in Hampstead.

The two Americans had waited half an hour that evening before Layton had arrived. He was carrying a large brown envelope which he laid carefully on the table, before he sat down to join them.

'First thing, Mr Kenny, I want you to look at these,' and he slid out four 10×8 photographs and laid them side by side on the table-top.

Hank Kenny leaned over and carefully studied them. After a few moments he looked up at Layton.

'The first, second and fourth I would identify as Lady

Hoult, the third I'm just not sure of. Something about the eyes that is different. Bigger maybe?'

Layton nodded. 'Well, that fits all right. The third one is Anita Ekberg at about the same age. The others *are* Hoult's wife, from three different sources.'

Layton looked across at the senior American.

'I've had a very quick analysis done on Hoult's public comments on the Russians. After-dinner speeches, broadcasts, newspaper interviews, and so on. And by a substantial margin they're more critical than favourable.'

'So what? The ones who really matter all do that. He's not going to advertise what he's up to.'

'Fair enough. So what do you think he *is* up to?'

'There's a wide range of possibilities. At most he's an agent, giving them whatever they want. He's in a better position than Philby. *His* stuff was top-level but it only covered security material. He'd got no access to Cabinet material. Next on the list he could just be using his influence, dropping in the right word for them when things were evenly balanced or going against them. Thirdly, he could just be giving a broad hint now and again. "Put the pressure on now" sort of stuff. You name it, he could be doing it.'

'Or maybe nothing? Just ambitious for that job. He'll almost certainly go to the House of Lords in the next year or two ...'

'Matt, the way things are going here there won't be a House of Lords in two years' time. You know that. All our reports indicate that you're very near boiling point over here. Hoult is in a key position to influence the Prime Minister. Just the man the Soviets would bust a gut to manipulate. He was in Moscow for three years or so, he's married to a Russian girl young enough to be his daughter who is known to have been closely associated with a KGB man who was used to get alongside diplomats. It stinks, Matt. There can't be any doubt.'

'I've ordered some checks in Moscow. These should be through later tonight.'

'Why don't you knock off Krasin? He must know what's

going on.'

'That would create a rare old stink.'

'Not so much as when you have to deal with Hoult, or when he skips to Moscow.' The stocky man stood up and shook himself to straighten his suit. 'You people do know what's going on here I take it. You've got the picture I hope. Roaring inflation, a million and a half unemployed *and* strikes. More public and private violence than any other country in Europe. Fellow-travellers in strategic positions in politics and the unions. A press that's running scared, and the man in the street getting on with his gardening, trying to pretend it isn't happening here. The chaos is going to increase, and when it does somebody's going to cash in on it and then they'll be yelling for help to Moscow – and that'll be it.'

Layton found no comfort in the fact that the American was echoing his own reports and evaluations for the last year. The politicians didn't want to hear it, and there's none so deaf as those who don't want to hear.

'I'll be staying here for a bit, Pete. I'll contact you as it develops.'

'OK, Matt. But remember, we're here to be used if you want us. Any resources the agency has are yours to use. Officially or unofficially, any way you want it.'

Pete Maddox was sorry for the Englishman. Since the end of the war they had been on a downhill path. The old empire gone, a colour problem they'd never had before, and now they were bled white economically, and no spirit to tackle the problems. He could imagine what it was like running SIS. Reporting subversion that your masters treated as evidence of democracy, violence that they called the will of the people, wilful and cruel disruption of the economic fabric that was called the redistribution of wealth. Maybe the Russians were what they deserved, but they weren't what the United States deserved, and they would be the next target for the Soviets. Ever since the final tragedy in South Vietnam, the United States' allies had started brushing up their Russian. The domino principle had cast its longest shadows across America's allies in Europe. It was every man for himself now.

When Krasin's conversation with Hoult had been relayed to Moscow, Andropov had fumed and sent Soloviev and a support team to the airport inside two hours. They had landed at de Gaulle in time for breakfast. Four had flown on to Dublin and Soloviev with two others had motored to Calais. They had landed, as day-trippers, in Dover early in the afternoon. Local party members would cover the return trip. They had waited at the house in Twickenham until the Dublin party had come over on the ferry. There had been no hitches.

Krasin had paid three months' rent in advance for a maisonnette in Mayfair's Queen Street and they had moved in two at a time after dark. Soloviev had walked around the area with Krasin, familiarizing himself with the streets and squares. They had been allowed to sleep until 6.30 the next morning.

After coffee and rolls Soloviev and Krasin had closed the big double doors that separated the sitting-room from the dining-room. They sat at the glass-topped table. Soloviev went over Krasin's conversation with Hoult, again and again. But there was no doubt that Hoult was not going to respond.

'Have you got any suggestion, Krasin?' Soloviev spoke with an air of irritation and impatience that did not encourage a response, and Krasin reacted accordingly. 'I would rather hear Moscow's views before I comment.'

'They want that report inside the next three days. We have already tried other leads to it but the SIS people have closed down as tight as a drum. Hoult is the only possible source. So how do we make him co-operate?'

Krasin had been involved in, or present at, too many discussions that started with those words not to know where they would lead. Despite the warmth and sunshine he felt suddenly cold. He looked up sharply at Soloviev, and said

112

softly, 'What have they got in mind?'

'The girl, his wife.'

'And we do what?'

'We can either kidnap her or threaten to eliminate her.'

Krasin's face was contorted with disbelief. 'If we killed her we might as well go back now. He was a soldier. A good record. He's a tough bastard. He'd have us torn to shreds in an hour.' He looked intently at Soloviev's grim face. 'If we killed her, Soloviev, Hoult would tell the world everything that had gone on. They wouldn't love him for his past, but by God our people over here would be absolutely finished. It would mark the end of the game.'

'So we kidnap her.'

Krasin bit the nicotine-stained flesh around his thumbnail as he tried to concentrate his mind. Soloviev interrupted. 'How do you think he would react?' Krasin ignored the question. His eyes were closed, his hands to his mouth. Soloviev had a brief picture of Krasin, those years ago, at the start of the operation. He'd sat like this then. Then Krasin stood up and walked slowly to the window. Across the road was a shop window, full of brightly coloured dresses and shirts.

In the last twenty years or so he had been responsible for people being imprisoned, tortured and, for a small number, killed. A few had been acquaintances, none had been friends. He didn't find it possible to contemplate the killing of Yelena. He couldn't do it himself and he doubted that he could even bear to be party to the planning. There were two experienced killers on the team so he would never need to know what had happened. But whether he went along with it or not, if they decided that only *that* would produce results quickly, then he had no doubt they would do it. Without regrets, and without compunction. His mind wouldn't concentrate, it slid from one diversion to another. He was turning back to face Soloviev when inspiration came.

'I think we've got to be very careful about doing anything to the girl. I think if she was harmed or kidnapped he

113

would react completely against us.'

Soloviev looked unimpressed. 'How do you work that out?'

'I think his reaction would be the opposite of what you expect. If we killed her he would have no incentive to co-operate, and if we kidnapped her I think he would have only one thing in mind – to destroy us. I don't think the Moscow affair is blackmail material, and he would be useless if we gave them proof that he had passed information to us. He made no real attempt to hide his relationship with Yelena in Moscow. And he said he knew what we were doing. He behaved like he had nothing to lose. I don't think he gave a damn about us exposing him. And it is to our advantage to get his co-operation beyond just these documents. That's not the end of the story for us.'

Soloviev shrugged irritably. 'So what do *you* suggest?'

'I suggest we kidnap his first wife, Adèle de Massu.'

There was a long silence as Soloviev looked at him with growing disbelief. 'You think he cares more about *her* than the girl?'

'No. Far from it. But involving the girl would send him berserk. Involving Adèle would prey on his guilt, make him feel responsible.'

Soloviev's face was still a mixture of doubt and surprise. And Krasin warmed to his theme.

'He takes his responsibilities to people seriously. He did with Yelena. He played ball with us out of a sense of fair play, and only incidentally out of fear of exposure. This is a wife. A wife he deserted without justification. For selfish reasons. And now because of him she's in danger. He's deeply and emotionally involved with Yelena. Touch her and he will react only by angry reflex. He's not emotionally involved with Adèle. He'll be calm enough to think, and he'll want to protect her, but calmly, with calculation. And in that frame of mind I'd guess he would do a deal.'

Soloviev looked intently at Krasin's face as if he could, by close examination, detect the validity of the arguments he had put forward.

'If Moscow agrees it would be you, Krasin, who would have to make it happen.'

Krasin sighed and shrugged slowly. 'So be it, comrade, so be it.'

It was past the PM's bed-time but he settled himself down to hear what Layton had to say. An odd man Layton, his reports were so critical of legislation, appointments and the PM's colleagues and associates, and yet he never seemed to be involved. Never enthusiastic, never the advocate, even the criticisms were not much more than comment. Like so many of his kind it had been Eton, Oxford and the Army. They looked thick, even sounded dull, but there was always the suspicion that inside the big frame and the big head was another man looking out and observing. He sipped at the glass of milk and slowly broke up the digestive biscuit as he read the report. Finally he looked up and Layton saw that his face was pale like dirty pastry that a child has played with. The PM slid the sheets across the shiny table-top.

'I've spoken with my deputy, the Foreign Secretary and the Attorney General. They all feel you should go ahead.'

Layton waited in the silence and then spoke quietly.

'And you, sir?'

'With much regret I agree. But I make one condition, and that will be paramount. Nobody will be charged or arrested unless you have sufficient evidence to satisy the DPP that he can bring a court case – and win.'

Layton shifted his bulky frame and the seat creaked under the strain.

'We could never meet that, Prime Minister. We couldn't have brought an ironclad case against Philby.'

'You're asking for a free hand then?'

'No, sir. All I ask is that we should be required to present evidence to the DPP that would satisfy him and the Attorney General that there was sufficient evidence to justify their arrest.'

When the Prime Minister sat silent, Layton leaned forward, and there was sympathy in his voice as he spoke. 'That way nobody could say afterwards that there were any special conditions. Neither prejudice in bringing charges, nor preference in consideration. That could be important afterwards, Prime Minister.'

The PM was shuffling biscuit crumbs into a small heap on the plate. He looked up slowly at Layton. 'You're quite right, Layton. We must think beyond the immediate problems. Go ahead on that basis.'

He stood up slowly and there was now a little colour in the podgy face. Who could tell, maybe he *would* still be in office dealing with the aftermath. The strong man who had shown neither fear nor favour. He had nodded a perfunctory dismissal to the SIS man and pressed the bell for his secretary.

Moscow had agreed and Krasin had flown to Amsterdam and then to Paris. He had taken a taxi to Quai Saint-Michel and then walked slowly to the Rue des Ecoles. He had stood outside the Larousse book shop for several minutes, staring at the statue of Montaigne, and then he had turned slowly and entered the shop. Ten minutes later he had paid for his copy of Servan-Schreiber's *Le défi américain* and he had chatted amiably to the young man who gave him his change. Even before Krasin had left the shop the young man was dialling a telephone number.

Half an hour later Krasin had strolled down the hall of the Sorbonne into the quiet courtyard. He walked on to the Galerie Richelieu, and a girl had come out of one of the classrooms. She had handed over the key with an amused smile, and he had thanked her and left.

Krasin walked back towards the river. At the corner of the Rue de la Huchette he stopped and looked across the river to the Île de la Cité where Notre-Dame cast its evening shadow along the Seine. But for all the filigree and the flying buttresses it didn't move his heart. It was too typically Paris, and its bulk too dark and ominous to be to the glory of Our Lady. It had that grim air of revenge and tragedy so common to medieval cathedrals, and so typical of his purpose in Paris.

He turned into the Rue de la Huchette and almost opposite the discothèque there was a heavy wooden door at the side of a pâtisserie. As he turned the key he was conscious of the warm smell of cooking sugar and caramel. The narrow stairs led up to a hallway with potted plants and a line of white-painted doors. He made for the second, and opened the door slowly and cautiously. When he stood in the centre of the big studio room the sun lit up the polished wooden furniture and caught the light footprints in the pile of the lime-green carpet.

Beneath the windows was boxed-in seating, painted white, with black foam cushions, and a sprawl of magazines. The prints on the walls were modern and there was an air of gaiety about the whole room. It was one of the KGB's Paris 'safe' houses. The youth in the Larousse shop lived there with his girl-friend from the Sorbonne.

Krasin sat down at the window seat, reached for the telephone, and dialled the special embassy number. They both spoke in Ukrainian and mentioned no names. The invitation had been accepted and the necessary arrangements had been made.

There had been a special recital with an invited audience at the Maison de la Radio, and the Russian Embassy had invited about fifty of the audience to a reception at the Embassy after the concert. Igor Oistrakh had not played in public in Paris since his father's death, and tonight he had played the Glazunov violin concerto and for an encore his own arrangement of the Bach Arioso. They didn't want to let him go, but finally he had smiled his way off the dais and walked through the velvet curtains.

The police were controlling the parking of the cars at the Embassy, and as the big Mercedes pulled up Krasin had held Adèle's arm as she stepped from the car. The Ambassador had paid her special attention, introducing her to the soloist and the leading musicians, and getting

them to autograph her programme. Krasin had stood, the
patient escort, bringing the champagne and canapés as she
chatted to the celebrities and her friends. There were greet-
ings too for Krasin himself.

It was nearly midnight as they walked around the Place
de l'Etoile, the traffic was still heavy, and the taxi drivers
all looked the other way. Adèle had her arm linked in his,
and when they stopped under one of the ornate street lights
he had put his arm around her.

'Let's go to my place and talk.'

She hesitated for only a moment. 'It's been a long time,
Viktor. Let's do that.'

They had finally got a taxi and it had dropped them in
the Place Saint-Michel.

She had admired the room and he had poured them
drinks. Sitting opposite her he had realized that she still
looked young for her forty years or more, and he had lifted
his glass with a smile. 'À toi, Adèle, jusqu'au bout de ma
vie.'

And she had laughed. 'You haven't changed, Viktor.
Still the eternal charmer.'

He nodded. 'And you. How is it with you?'

She shrugged. 'On existe, Viktor, on existe.'

'No new husband?'

She shook her head and her face was sad. 'No. I'm afraid
not.'

'But many men, I'm sure.'

'A few, but just men, just friends.'

'And still the hurt.'

She hesitated, sipping her drink. 'Regret more than hurt.'

'Regret for what? The man? The life?'

She sighed. 'Talking to you is like reminiscing with
enemies after a war.'

'I was never an enemy, Adèle. Never that.'

'Not consciously maybe, although I'm not sure even
about that. You were the catalyst that made everything
change.'

'You miss him still?' He saw the tears at the edge of her eyes.

'I miss him of course, but the pain is for my stupidity.'

He lit them cigarettes and she leaned forward to take hers from him, and used the movement to cover the hand that touched her eyes.

'Tell me.'

'I regret that I only really understood him when it was too late. Maybe all ex-wives say this, but in my case it is true. It would be easier if I could feel aggrieved, but I can't, because I was blind and stupid.' She sighed, put down her glass and looked at Krasin. 'Even that isn't true, Viktor. I think I really knew all the time. And I pretended not to notice. It hurt me when it happened, it hurts me still. But my God I must have hurt him a dozen times a day, every day of our lives.'

Krasin sat silent and still, and she went on, as if she were thinking aloud.

'If ever a man's life was ruined by other people it was Jamie's. He never had a choice all his life. Right from the start, people or circumstances forced him to be something. He never chose, it always seemed inevitable. And God knows he always did his best. He always succeeded. If there had been no war he might have escaped his fate. If there had been no *me* he might have escaped his fate.'

Krasin poured her another drink and as she lifted the glass she shivered and went on.

'His education was poor and he had no chance to develop later. He had to be a soldier – and he was a good one. He stayed half a soldier in military government. He married me, so the family made him a banker. Because he had no qualifications nobody asked *him* what he wanted to be. And because he was always so good at jumping the hurdles, we all took it for granted that he didn't mind. He had courage enough, but we all used it up in a thousand trivialities. He must have felt like a performing animal all the time he was married to me. The stupid social round that I was good

119

at – all that nonsense, and he said so many times how much he disliked it, and I never listened because *I* liked it.'

She gulped back the brandy and the glass rattled down on the table as she leaned back. 'Have you seen him since it all happened, Viktor?'

'Yes, Adèle, I saw him in New York recently, and I saw him in London a few days ago.'

'How is he?'

He hesitated and she laughed harshly. 'The truth, Viktor.'

'I think he is happy. It's hard to tell,' he said softly.

'And you? How have you survived?'

'Maybe not the Party's favourite son but I survive, my dear. No real problems.'

'And who is your current lady love? Do I know her?'

He smiled and shook his head. 'A playmate or two but nothing more.'

She smiled at him. 'And now I must go, Viktor. It's late.'

He looked at her and sighed, and shook his head.

'I'm afraid not, my dear.'

She half laughed in surprise and made to stand up. 'What's the matter, Viktor. What's going on?'

The soft brown eyes looked at hers as they had looked once before, at the Embassy in Moscow.

'There is a problem, Adèle. A problem we have with Jamie. We have to use you as a pressure point.' He shrugged. 'I'm terribly sorry, and I assure you you'll come to no harm. You just have to stay here with me.'

Her face was pale and her eyes tormented. She said softly, 'You mean you're using me to threaten Jamie?'

He nodded. 'Exactly.'

For a moment she seemed transfixed, and then she buried her face in her hands and sobbed. She looked up at Krasin, her face wet with tears. 'Why me? Why not Yelena?'

'His reactions for her would be unthinking. About you he will think. And we think he will co-operate.'

She rocked herself backwards and forwards in the chair, a reflex to her tensions, the tears still streaming down her face. She shuddered as a crying child shudders.

'My God, my God, how he must hate us all.'

'I don't think he's a hater, Adèle.'

'He will be now. He must treasure his life with Yelena. He's not young any more.' She looked up at Krasin. 'Did *you* work this out, Viktor?'

'Yes, I did. The alternative was something much worse.'

'And you expect me to co-operate for Auld Lang Syne.'

'I beg you to co-operate for all our sakes. Yours, Jamie's, mine and —' He didn't finish.

'— and Yelena's.'

'Yes.'

CHAPTER ELEVEN

Layton had had lengthy discussions with the DPP officials to review the results of the liaison between the SIS teams and the DPP teams. The Attorney General had arrived for the meeting that would approve, or otherwise, the first part of the SIS operation. He had seen the files and the legal notes, and had had a difficult conversation with the PM who was having second thoughts.

Sir Lincoln Evans had represented one of the Midlands constituencies since 1960 and was sure enough of his political base to be immune from constituency or parliamentary pressures. He was always prepared to listen, but he operated pretty much by the book. With three generations of lawyers behind him he was never in doubt where his loyalties lay. They were with the law and the judiciary. He had rather a brusque manner with a tendency to assume that ignorance of the law was either deliberate or a sign of low intelligence. He was feared by some, loathed by a few, but accepted as totally honest by all concerned with making and administering the law of the land.

He sat down at the table with something of a bustle and flipped open the catches on his leather case with such familiarity that he could afford to look around at the others as he did so. He lifted out the first few file covers. As he opened the top one his long forefinger scratched the side of his mouth and he looked sharply at Layton.

'Well now, Mr Layton, I've sorted these out in quotas of importance. Not importance from a security point of view but the importance of the people concerned. What I would call the pandemonium factor.' He leaned back, digging a probing finger into various waistcoat pockets. 'I couldn't give your department very good marks for this little lot.' He waved a bony hand at the files. 'Not even for neatness. However, let's have a look at what we have. Let's take these four here. A top TUC man. Two Ministers of the Crown and a senior adviser to the PM. Let us take them in that order.' He stopped for a moment as if seeking the others' approval. Nobody around the table made any sign of either agreement or disagreement.

'Frank O'Hara. Member of the TUC Council. Secretary of one of the largest unions. Millions of members. So what do we have? Member of Communist Party since the Spanish Civil War. Now I ask you, Layton, if that were incriminatory you'd have half the Cabinet and half the party in Wormwood Scrubs. Documents that show he has been receiving £2,000 a month through the Czech Embassy. Since when has that been an offence? When I was practising I had a large retainer from the Polish Government for advice on contracts. Does that make me suspect?' He looked sharply at Layton.

'It would if you were paid in cash, on the bridge in St James's Park, at the Odeon Leicester Square, and through a porn bookshop in Victoria.'

Evans shook his head. 'Afraid not, dear boy. Unorthodox maybe, suspicious maybe, but not, I'm afraid, illegal on any count.

'Then we have all these meetings with KGB officers. Can you imagine what defence counsel would do? Well I'll tell you. He'll want your proof that they *are* KGB. And when you've proved it to *your* satisfaction he'll pull the chain on you, and ask you why they are still here if they are up to their tricks. If you arrest them *too* you'll have an international incident and they will lie like flat fish. These men must meet dozens of quite innocent people in the course of their duties. Are *they* all suspect too?' He stretched his arms as if he were wearing a gown. 'And then the days lost in strikes in his union. Most of them are unofficial so he will say he was against them. And these transcripts of broadcasts defending the wild-cat strikes. Useless. Of course he will defend them, may*be* for subversive reasons, but defending counsel would point out that he's got to live with these people when the strike's over. He's paid to protect their interests even when he doesn't agree with their views.' He pushed the file aside. 'He's not a starter, Layton.'

'He had a meeting with a KGB major yesterday. They met at the Tate Gallery.'

'And?'

'And we arrested the KGB man later. He had documents affecting national security.'

'What documents?'

'There was an outline plan for organizing a total work stoppage in the Midlands, a regional general strike. A plan for one of the print unions to stop the national dailies from being printed, and a list of MPs who would co-operate with the trade unions in petitioning the PM for the suspension of Parliament.'

'Why was I not told about this?'

'We have only just finished making various checks on the documents. Comparing signatures and so on.'

Evans leaned back in his chair and his pale blue eyes looked sharply at Layton. 'However, you took a risk when you picked up the KGB man. You were "fishing", not acting on evidence?'

'We saw material pass.'

'What form was all this in?'

'A microfiche. Five inches by four inches. A piece of film. It was inside a catalogue.'

'Have you taken any additional action against the two Ministers?'

'Only full-time surveillance.'

'And Sir James Hoult?'

'The same.'

'In the case of Hoult I think you're on very thin ice. He has deceived his colleagues regarding his wife's nationality He obviously deliberately misled the security people. A case for dismissal certainly, but it would cause more uproar than it's worth, I should say.' There was a query in his

124

voice and in his lifted eyebrows.

'We think there could have been documents passed to the Soviets.'

'You say that about the Ministers.'

'It's one of the three and we think now it may be Hoult.'

'Why him?'

'There have been strong indications of top-level leaks on a wide variety of sensitive subjects. Until we got the information about Hoult's wife the two Ministers were suspect because the leaks concerned their ministries. Hoult has access to the same material as the PM. He could supply the Soviets with anything they want.'

'He's never appeared to be pro-Soviet. Got a reputation for sound advice.'

'You couldn't have better cover than that, Sir Lincoln.'

Evans looked around the table and then back at Layton. 'I think we should have a word on our own.'

When the others had gone Evans lit a cigar and leaned forward with his arms on the table. 'Did the PM give you any special instructions, Layton?'

'Just that we should go ahead with the round-up but we should satisfy the DPP that there was a case.'

'Nothing *more* than that?'

'He went further than that in discussion but not in his final instructions.'

'You're using Special Branch for the arrests, are you?'

'All procedure is absolutely standard.'

'When will this break so far as the media are concerned?'

'Not for several days. We are picking off the other side first.'

'Any trouble with the Foreign Office on that score?'

'Not so far.'

Evans stood up and loaded the files into his case. As he leaned over he looked up at Layton.

'I'm not going over this in detail, Layton. I think you know what you're doing, and I'm sure you know the pitfalls. Bear in mind that by Tuesday or Wednesday there'll certainly be strong demands for an Emergency Debate in the House.'

They had been to the cinema on their own. It was a rerun of *Le Bonheur* in a double bill with *Un homme et une femme* and they had come out blinking into the sunshine of Leicester Square. They had taken a taxi to Belgrave Square and then walked to the flat.

Hoult had walked over to the hi-fi and had slid in the cassette of Strauss Waltzes. He had turned round to speak to Yelena and saw that her face was white, and she was shivering.

'What is it, Yelena? What's the matter?'

She put a finger to her teeth to stop them from chattering, and she looked up at him as she whispered 'The man, Jamie. The man.'

'What man.'

'He was standing in the doorway of the antique shop. And he was outside the cinema when we came out. He's KGB, Jamie.'

Hoult walked over to the window and standing against the wall he cautiously looked out. There *was* a man there, he was looking at his watch, and he looked like a typical KGB thug. Still against the wall he said, 'What makes you think he's KGB, love?'

She shuddered. 'He is, Jamie. I am quite sure.'

Hoult was reaching for the phone when it rang. He picked up the receiver slowly and cautiously and gave the number.

'Sir James Hoult?'

'Speaking.'

'Mr Krasin asked me to speak to you, Sir James.'

'Yes.'

'He asked if you could help with the problem he mentioned to you.'

'I've already given him my answer. It's no. And I suggest you remove your little man who is following me about. If he's still around in an hour's time I shall call the police.'

126

'Mr Krasin said that he would be prepared to do a deal with you, Sir James. He suggests ...'

And Hoult had hung up.

A black embassy car had pulled up fifteen minutes later and picked up the man from the corner shop.

A packet had flopped on to the parquet floor in the hall about 2 a.m. Nobody had heard it arrive.

Yelena sat wrapped in her dressing gown as Hoult put the cassette into the hi-fi. There were a few seconds of silence and then a click and what was unmistakably Krasin's voice.

'I'm sorry about this, Jamie, but it has to be done. We need this information very quickly. Adèle is with me and is quite safe for the moment. However I have had certain instructions. If you doubt my statement please telephone her home number and check. Please be very discreet. We do not want to worry her friends unnecessarily. Please understand that my influence is limited. We require the information in the next twenty-four hours. As soon as it is available phone the contact number and ask for Soloviev. He will give you instructions. If he has not heard from you by 9 a.m. tomorrow the responsibility for what happens to Adèle will be yours. And then there would be pressures on others that I could not stop. There will be no other contacts so I leave it in your hands.'

Yelena looked across at Hoult as the tape ran on in silence, then the auto-stop clicked and the red light came on. His eyes were looking at her but she knew he didn't see her.

Hoult's thoughts would not leave that final threatening phrase – '... then there would be pressures on others ...' They must mean the boys and Yelena. But Piers and Blair were both in the States. They were hitch-hiking across to the West Coast. Even *he* couldn't contact them, so the Russians couldn't either. So they must only mean Yelena. He had no other hostages to fortune, no other pressure point. He stood up slowly and then smiled at the girl. 'Pack

127

a bag for us, Yelena, I must make some phone calls, and then we'll be on our way.'

Hoult had booked them a suite in another name at the Hilton, and after they had settled in he had gone down in the elevator to the foyer.

He moved over to an armchair facing the main entrance and watched carefully as the taxis dropped their passengers outside. After half an hour he walked over to the paper kiosk and bought an early edition of the *Evening Standard*. There was a thick black headline across the front page – 'The PM Acts' it said, in type three inches high. There was a row of photographs of half a dozen people taken into custody, and a largish photograph of the Prime Minister getting into his car outside Number Ten. He had started reading the small amount of copy when he saw Layton walk through the revolving doors, down the steps and past reception. He stood up and followed slowly behind him up to the first floor.

The tables were laid for morning coffee and the pianist was playing a selection from *Salad Days*. There was a fair sprinkling of mid-morning shopping ladies, and a few groups of businessmen with brief cases bulging and files jostling the crockery.

Layton had headed for a table against the wall and as Hoult approached he pointed to an empty chair. He waved his big fist at a waiter and ordered coffee for the two of them.

'We'd better wait till the fellow has finished bringing the coffee.' He looked around the restaurant. 'Amazin' how many people have time to hang around in places like these in the middle of the morning.'

'Probably tourists, Layton,' Hoult had said, with a dry smile. He was used to the Laytons of this world. They weren't really as archaic as they pretended.

The waiter slid the tray on to the table and laid the bill in front of Hoult, who pushed it on one side. He poured coffee for them both and handed Layton the sugar.

'I have a problem, Layton. In your sort of area. I thought we should talk.'

Layton raised his eyebrows and nodded. 'Go right ahead, Sir James.' He eased himself back in his seat like a badger backing into its sett. He looked at his coffee to avoid Hoult's pale blue eyes.

'I understand that there's some sort of security sweep going on at the moment. I saw a headline in the newspaper, but I was told about it a couple of days ago.'

Layton's head came up and he looked over the top of his cup. 'Who told you a couple of days ago – the PM?'

'No. He hasn't mentioned it at all. The man who told me is a Russian – one of their officials.'

Layton put his cup down slowly. 'And who might he be, Sir James?'

'His name is Krasin. Viktor Krasin. I knew him in Moscow. He's a very well-known Soviet actor. I think he is also an officer in the KGB.'

Layton's arms were sprawled across the arms of his chair and his body looked relaxed as he sat with his non-committal face. He was silent as he waited for Hoult to continue.

'He told me that his superiors in Moscow had wind of a round-up of fellow travellers and the like.' Hoult waited for a response.

'And?'

'And he asked for my help.'

'What kind of help?'

'He wanted details of the security operation.'

'Why should he ask you?'

'Several reasons, Layton. I was Ambassador in Moscow as you know, and Krasin knew me at that time. Also he had certain information about me that he thought would ;mbarrass me. During the night they put a packet through my door. It was one of those small cassette things. It's a recorded message from Krasin. They've kidnapped my first wife.'

'Have you checked on this?'

'There is no answer from her Paris number.'

'You want us to liaise with the French on this?'

'Rather more than that. There is a contact number that they want me to use. I would be willing to contact these people so that you can deal with them.'

'And the deal?'

'I want protection for my wife.'

Layton sat looking at Hoult and there was a long silence but Hoult was not moved to speak again. And finally Layton had leaned forward and he had said quietly, 'And *your* loyalties, Sir James, where do those lie?'

Hoult's half-smile drew down one corner of his mouth. 'My loyalties are to my wife, Layton. And I have responsibilities to my former wife but I will take care of those. All I ask from you is protection for my wife.'

'And for yourself?'

Hoult shook his head slowly and his face was grim. 'I ask nothing for me. Nothing at all.'

'D'you know the name of your contact.'

'Yes. It's a man named Soloviev.'

'Do you know him?'

'No. Not unless I met him in Moscow.'

'He's well known to us. A full colonel in the KGB. A subversion specialist.'

'There is a time limit on this.'

'How long?'

'Twenty-four hours is what it says on the cassette, and we got that this morning.'

'Can you come back to my office, Sir James?'

'What about protection for my wife?'

'Where is she?'

'Here in the hotel.'

Layton stood up slowly, his eyes on Hoult's face as he said slowly, 'She's entitled to our help, Sir James. Just like any other British citizen. I will phone my people and we will wait until someone arrives.'

They had walked to the telephone by the cloakroom, and Hoult had stood aloof as Layton spoke on the telephone.

They walked down again to the foyer and sat together on one of the big settees. Almost twenty minutes later Layton had turned and said, 'My man is here now, Sir James. We can leave. I shall not keep you long.'

'Will your man recognize my wife?'

The smile was barely noticeable as Layton nodded. 'He'll know her all right. He won't make contact unless it's essential.'

An official car had been waiting on the forecourt and they were at the building in Petty France in ten minutes.

Lucas and his team sat in the darkened projection room. There was a dim light on the lectern and Layton's face looked eerie from the low-level lighting. He raised his hand and the curtains slowly parted on the big screen, a motor purring smoothly, and suddenly the screen was bright from the projector. Layton coughed and started.

'We have very little briefing time so leave your questions to the end.' He turned slightly as the pictures came up. 'This is Sir James Hoult. There is a 'P' file for each of you to read later. Not a bad-looking face actually, reminiscent of somebody but I can't think who. There ...'

'David Niven.' It was Lucas who interrupted.

'You're right, John. Now here is full length – and here he is alongside the PM, much the same height – ah, now this is a profile and here is his current passport photograph – copies of this have gone to the ports and airports – here he is with his wife. Here is a full face of his wife – she speaks English, French and Russian, that was missed from the typed notes – Robins and Mathews will be responsible for her protection, and her surveillance.

'This is Soloviev, there is a lot of material on him and a précis has been done for you that covers the relevant material. He is very experienced. Has operated in the United States and was at the London Embassy for two years in charge of "legals". It seems, from the instructions that Hoult has received, that Soloviev is in this country, probably in London. There is no record of his arrival in

131

that name, and he is not on the embassy staff, not even under an alias.

'Hoult is going to telephone this number, Signals Security will be trying a trace, but in any case he will agree to passing the documents under whatever arrangements they suggest. He will try to stretch the time factor before handing over so that we can plan your part of the operation as well as possible.

'You will be instructed to take into custody anybody who seems connected with the pick-up. There is a file on known Soviet dead-letter drops in London but I doubt if they will use those. So. I can't spend much time on answering questions. As you know, I'm much occupied at the moment.'

The lights came on and Layton stood at the side of the lectern, his eyebrows raised interrogatively. There was silence for a few moments and then someone spoke.

'Is there any chance that the pick-up could test the documents before continuing the operation, and find them wanting, and cut off at that point?'

'No chance at all. Well, let me be more precise. The documents will be entirely authentic so he would be making an error rather than being cautious if he cut out the operation at the pick-up point. The documents will not be complete of course, but even a check with the newspapers will show that they cover accurately what is already public knowledge.'

Lucas stood up and looked along the row of chairs at his team.

'I'll answer anything else you want to ask. The chief has other things to do.' He looked across at Layton. 'Thank you, sir.'

Back at the Hilton Hoult sat reading the evening edition of the *Standard*. There was a much fuller report of the security sweep and even without much information on actual names it was obvious that the operation was much bigger than the first edition had indicated. The editorial left no doubt that the paper was in complete agreement with the Prime Minister.

As the news comes in from all parts of the country of suspects being picked up by the police and Special Branch, it is obvious that the Prime Minister's courageous action has the full support of the general public.

Never since the referendum on the EEC has this newspaper received so many telephone calls from its readers in support of government action.

For too long it has been apparent that in Parliament, the trade unions, and even in the media itself, there have been people of influence who have had a vested interest in damaging this country's hard-earned reputation for industrial efficiency, political tolerance and freedom of choice and speech.

We have seen the big battalions march roughshod over the rest of the working population, seizing on any excuse to disrupt our lives and to set class against class.

Already there are signs that the extreme left still hope to serve the interests of their masters in Moscow by challenging the authority of the Government and the Prime Minister, but on behalf of our readers we send them this message loud and clear – THE GAME IS UP, COMRADES.

Hoult looked down the list of names of those who were in custody. There were few surprises for him, but for the general public the list would seem almost unbelievable. Members of Parliament, three Junior Ministers, twenty civil servants, novelists, actors, two TV personalities, an editor and a dozen journalists, a handful of trade union leaders and deputies, and a list of unknowns like a World War I casualty list.

There was talk of left-wing demonstrations to be arranged to march on Downing Street and the Houses of Parliament. An application for an Emergency Debate. The Soviet Embassy windows were being boarded up and the *Morning Star* had ceased publication. All services leave and police leave had been cancelled and troops were being flown back to Brize Norton from Ulster. The BBC and ITV were breaking into all programmes with news flashes. The Prime Minister was broadcasting to the nation at 8 o'clock.

He put the paper down beside his chair and looked across at the bed. Yelena lay under the thin coverlet, asleep, with her blonde hair spread over the pillows like fronds of seaweed on an incoming tide. He walked over, and as he sat on the bed she opened her eyes and leaned up on one elbow, and with her other hand she arranged her hair. Even though she was still half asleep she smiled at him, and he was terribly aware of her beauty. The vivid blue eyes, the pert nose, the soft full lips and the white teeth that her upper lip could never cover.

The narrow black moiré band at her wrist emphasized the pale roundness of her arms, and as he smiled at her she reached out for him. Her softness cradled against him and his hands stroked her back, and as he leaned back to look at her face the coverlet slid away to uncover one of her breasts. She smiled as he pulled the smooth golden satin away from her, and as he drew the coverlet aside she lay back smiling as he looked at her body. She watched as he undressed and turned eagerly to him as he lay alongside her, his hands closing over the smooth, firm flesh of her breasts.

They were asleep when the phone rang and as Hoult came awake his hand moved round on the side table in the darkness. It was Layton. 'We should like you to phone him now, Sir James. If we wait too long they might be suspicious. We have removed the set of documents from the PM's office so that if they have some means of checking the story it will stand up. Good luck.'

'Thank you, Layton.' His voice was flat and in the darkness he felt a moment's fear. The dark room seemed like a lost world, not a haven, but a transit camp on the way to some dreadful fate. He shivered, and as his eyes grew more used to the light he put his hand on the girl, on the shadowy triangle between her long legs. He leaned over and kissed her awake.

He had drawn the curtains and dressed, and while Yelena

134

was bathing he asked the operator for the number. Layton had thought that that would give authenticity.

The phone shrilled and the hotel operator said, 'Your number, caller.'

'Soloviev?'

'Speaking, Sir James.'

'I have the papers you wanted.'

'Excellent. Where are you speaking from?'

'The Hilton Hotel.'

'I see. Have you a room there?'

'Yes.'

'What number is it?'

'1704.'

'I'll call you back.'

'It's not in my name.'

'I will ask for the room then,' and he had hung up.

Two minutes later the phone had rung again.

'Sir James?'

'Yes?'

'You know the Festival Hall, Sir James?'

'Very well.'

'Good, you will collect two tickets for your wife and yourself at the ticket office. They are for Box G. Box G for Golf. The other seats in the box will not be taken. The seats are paid for. You will take the papers and leave them under the first chair. The extreme left-hand chair. The chair nearest the stage. At the interval you will leave. If everything is satisfactory we shall contact you at the hotel about ten o'clock this evening. We will have notified our friend in Paris, and we shall make arrangements for the lady to confirm to you that she is at liberty. Is this understood?'

'Yes. Box G. Extreme left-hand seat. Leave at the interval.'

'Correct.'

Hoult looked at his watch. Layton had said wait ten minutes before phoning unless the arrangements made it impossible.

It was five minutes later when the phone rang again. 'A

call for you, sir.'

'Who is that?'

There was a pause, and then the phone clicked and was dead. Like Layton had said, they had phoned back to check if he was using the phone.

He had asked for room-service from the operator and Layton's man Lucas had arrived in minutes. He had listened carefully to the instructions given to Hoult and then he had left. He had instructed Hoult to do exactly what he was told to do by Soloviev, and to come back to the hotel. They were to take the third taxi in the rank at the Festival Hall. The driver would say 'Hello Jamie'.

'You won't try anything silly, Adèle, will you?'

'Like what?'

'Oh, shouting for help. Trying to get away. That sort of thing. It would be really bad for all of us if you were foolish.'

'Tell me something, Viktor.'

'What?'

'Has Jamie co-operated with your people since he's been back in London?'

He shrugged 'Comme ci, comme ça. He has helped us, but nothing very important.'

'And you think he will co-operate now because of me.'

'I'm sure he will.'

'But why?'

'He felt guilty about the divorce, and all that. He feels responsible for you and he'll feel especially responsible for this situation.'

'I think you've gone too far this time.'

She could see the doubt in his eyes. The first realization that they could have misjudged the situation. She spoke as if she *knew*, not as if it were conjecture. She was sitting on the edge of the bed and he sat down slowly beside her, looking intently at her face.

'Tell me why you think that, Adèle.'

'Jamie can be persuaded. He can be drawn along, but

136

whenever people put his back to the wall he breaks away. Look what happened when the pressure was on in Moscow. I never knew what happened but I'm sure he didn't do what your people expected.'

She could tell from his face that she was right, and she waited in silence for him to react. His fingers picked at the fringe of the bed-cover and then he looked up at her face. She was very beautiful still, and the curve of her face and the line of her jaw were still those of a young girl. And the big brown eyes were as clear and alive as they had been that night at the Embassy. She wasn't the kind you could bluff. He said very quietly, 'What on earth shall we do, Adèle?'

'What were you told to do?'

His eyes were on her face and he hesitated for several seconds. 'I would have to kill you, Adèle. Those were my orders.'

He could see the pulse beating at her slender throat. 'And how would you kill me, my dear?' And when she had said 'my dear' it had had no ring of a jibe.

He shook his head, sharing her disbelief. 'I have a gun.'

She looked at the troubled handsome face and shared his emptiness. The emptiness of a loser.

'Could you do it, Viktor?'

There were tears in his eyes as he shook his head. 'No, Adèle. I would sooner kill myself. But that may not save you from the others.'

'Why did you ever get mixed up with the KGB?'

He shrugged. 'It helped my career. It gave me opportunities to meet influential people, and I got many privileges that way. It was OK when I was young, but these days it's not good.'

'Why?'

'I don't know. Just age maybe. I want a quiet life.'

'Why don't you leave then?'

He laughed harshly. 'Adèle, my dear, you don't leave the KGB. Maybe they throw you out, but you don't leave.'

'I meant, why don't you leave Russia?'

She knew from his slow reaction that this wasn't the first

time the thought had been in his mind.

'Where do I stay? What do I do?'

'You could stay in France, and you could earn a living as an actor, or something in the theatre.'

He smiled. 'Don't worry, Adèle. I won't have to kill you. Jamie will do as he is told.'

She shook her head. 'I assure you he will not. He will go for your people.'

'If he does that it would be *finis* for all of us.'

'If he does do that, will you let me help you make a new life here, Viktor?'

He looked at her intently, and suddenly they were no longer fencing and probing. 'They would get me, Adèle. They would kill me.'

'They wouldn't dare. If you were just a KGB man maybe they would. But not as a public figure. They value the French *détente* more than that.'

He stood up and she could see that he looked uneasy and disturbed. 'Let us see what happens.'

'But if it turns out like I say, you would do it?'

He sighed and held out his arms like any Frenchman. 'I would have no choice, Adèle. I couldn't kill you, that's for sure, and if I went back I would be finished even if I wasn't killed. If it happens like you say I will consider what we do.' Then he snapped out of the gloomy mood. 'Let's have a drink before we eat, my dear.'

The phone rang as he poured the drinks and he stood listening intently, his teeth biting on his lower lip. Then he nodded. 'Ya gatov, spasebo.' And he slowly replaced the receiver as he looked at Adèle.

'You were wrong, thank God. Jamie has contacted them and has agreed to co-operate.'

She looked back at him and reached for her drink.

'Don't rely on it, Viktor.'

'You seem very sure.'

'I *am* very sure.'

CHAPTER TWELVE

Lucas had placed his team well in advance at the Festival Hall and had kept in constant radio contact. He could see Box G as he watched with binoculars from the projection room. Apart from Hoult and his wife, nobody had entered the box during the overture or the Rachmaninov. It was Neville Marriner and the Northern Symphony, and the Festival Hall was less full than they deserved. But the applause was thunderous as the house lights came up for the interval.

He saw the Hoults stand, and then leave the box. The binoculars were resting on a projection stand as he kept them trained steadily on Box G. The orchestra were reassembling for the second half of the programme when the woman entered the box. He saw her stoop, then stand up and leave the box.

Then the radio traffic came in almost continuously. The woman had gone into the toilets and had come out a few minutes later. The envelope flap was open and they guessed she had made the first check. She had walked slowly along the river embankment and meanwhile the toilets had been searched but nothing was found. The woman had continued to the car park and had driven off towards Waterloo Station. The car number was being checked by the central control unit back at Petty France. At the roundabout she turned left on to Waterloo Bridge. She headed on towards the Strand and by the time she was at Trafalgar Square one of Lucas's cars was three cars behind her.

A second car was waiting at Green Park and a third covered Berkeley Square. The third car had covered her to the Hilton car park and a pair of observers had trailed her down to Shepherd Market where she walked through to Curzon Street and back along to the cinema. There was a queue for the new Fellini, and as the girl walked past the lines of people a man on the inside file waved to her, and she excused herself to the people near him and joined him in the crowd.

There were three observers now, one at each end of the short street, and Lucas standing near the cinema entrance. As the couple neared the head of the queue Lucas knew that the man was not one of the regulars from the Embassy but he had seen photographs of the girl before. He couldn't remember her name but he remembered that she was a student at the London School of Economics; she was on file as a known associate of an Irishman who had paid frequent visits to meet Czech arms-dealers in Amsterdam. There was no sign now of the thick brown envelope.

Inside the cinema the couple had sat together, watching the last fifteen minutes of the main film and then the lights had gone up. The man had stood up and walked towards the sign that said 'Toilets'. He had stayed there until the main lights had gone down and then he had walked slowly up to the exit. It was impossible to use the radio control to the watchers inside the cinema, but they had a standard routine. Someone had stayed watching the girl and a burly man had followed the Irishman.

He had circled the byways of Shepherd Market a few times and then crossed Curzon Street to Queen Street. He had bought a stamp from the slot machine outside the Post Office and had then walked up to the end of the street. He looked at the shirts and dresses in the Mary Davies shop, and then looked up and down the street. When the street was clear of people he sauntered across the road and as he walked up the three low steps the street door opened from inside and he walked in.

Lucas had radioed back to main control to see if he could get details of the building.

'Try the GLC planning department, or one of the big estates. Probably Cadogan or Westminster.'

'It's Saturday night, chief, they won't be around.'

'It's always bloody Saturday. Any other ideas?'

' 'Fraid not. What's it look like?'

'Looks like a private house.'

'What's next door like?'

'A twin, except for the colour. That's got a solicitor's plate up.'

'How long can you wait?'

'Why?'

'I can send a lock boy round and he could let you have a look around inside the one next door.'

'How long before he gets here?'

'Five minutes, maybe ten.'

'OK. Let's do that.'

Lucas had pulled his net around Queen Street and there didn't appear to be a back entrance or a garden, but the house backed on to a club and there could be a way through.

A taxi flashed its headlights near the zebra crossing in Curzon Street and Lucas walked on down. The locksmith was ex-Portsmouth police, and after he had listened to Lucas's instructions he'd walked up Queen Street with a girl who stood with him on the steps of the solicitor's offices. They had both gone inside a few minutes later. Lucas and one of his team had walked down from the top end of the street. The door was ajar and they went inside.

They spent ten minutes checking the layout of the three floors. The conversion to offices had not been well done and the shape of the original rooms was still visible.

Lucas had called in all his team except the man trailing the girl and one observer in Queen Street. He had his hand half over the head of the torch, and they sat on desks as he briefed them.

'None of these boys gets away. You understand that. I want them in custody. I genuinely want them alive, preferably in one piece. They're important and they will provide us with a lot of information. If we're careful we could even use them as witnesses. But. If necessary you shoot. If they're armed and even make a move to a gun, you shoot. No warnings. If anyone gets loose beyond the boys who'll be in the street you shoot at fifteen feet. The boys outside

141

will *not*, repeat *not*, use silencers, or you'll miss 'em. If we get split up for any reason you head back to Petty France. If by any chance you get picked up by the police, show your warrant card but don't give any explanations. You refer them to Layton personally. If he's not around they should refer to the duty officer at either Special Branch or Petty France. Any questions?'

'How many are there and any idea who they are? Identification I mean.'

'No idea on either count but I'd guess that Soloviev will be among those present. And that bloody Irishman, of course.'

'O'Malley.'

'That's it. Couldn't remember the bastard's name.'

He held up his hand and adjusted the plastic ear-plug.

'The girl's left the cinema, heading for the Hilton. I doubt if she'll be coming this way.' He stood up and made for the door. 'Burrows, you do the door for us if you can. We might surprise 'em.'

The Irishman had been half-way down the stairs when Burrows opened the door. For a split second he looked paralysed with disbelief, and then he had turned, shouting, and had headed back up the stairs. The first man had caught one leg, and the big Irishman had flailed his arms to grab the stair-rail, and, missing, had curved over backwards, his head banging each step until he lay still and inert against the door.

Lucas by this time was at the top of the stairs and turned left into a room with lights on. Two men were standing looking out of the window. One of them was Soloviev and he turned quickly, his face flushed with anger.

'What the hell is this? Who are you?'

'The police, Mr Soloviev. Don't move.'

Soloviev instinctively moved his hand towards his chest, and then cried out as he clutched his elbow and a wisp of smoke curled from the silencer of Lucas's pistol.

The other man lifted his hands high and somebody put

him with his face to the wall.

They had rounded up five men and were back at the studios in Pimlico ten minutes later. They were a man short but they didn't know it.

One of Layton's men who had been left behind picked up two men who came along later. They were both from the Russian Embassy and Layton released them just before midnight.

There had been no call for Hoult at ten o'clock but about two in the early morning he had heard from Layton that his men had made Soloviev phone through to Krasin at a Paris number and he had given instructions for Adèle to be released immediately. A fluent Russian speaker had monitored the call and confirmed that the instructions had been given.

Krasin sat slowly back into his chair with his head in his hands and Adèle had pleaded with him. 'What's wrong, Viktor? What did he say?'

Krasin looked up, red-eyed with exhaustion, his face drawn taut from fatigue and tension.

'It was Soloviev, the man in charge. He ordered me to release you.'

'Why are you so worried then?'

'He was speaking under duress. They must have picked him up.'

'How could you tell?'

'He made it clear in what he said.'

'Tell me, Viktor. Tell me quickly before it's too late.'

'He said that Hoult had co-operated so I should release the girl. But instead of saying *devushka* he said *devka*.'

'What's the difference?'

'Oh God. *Devushka* is the proper word, the correct word, for 'girl'. *Devka* is slang like 'chick' or 'babe'. It's a standard way of indicating that you're under duress. All service messages have to be correct and formal. It's cast-iron procedure. He was warning me.' He looked at Adèle's white

143

face. 'Christ, what *do* we do?'

'We collect our things and we leave Paris right now.'

'Where shall we go?'

'I've got a cottage in Honfleur. We'll go there.'

'You'll be traced too easily.'

'No. I've only just rented it for six months. Nobody will know.'

'How do we get there?'

'We'll take a taxi to the Place Vendôme and telephone the Hertz office for a hire car. We can telephone from the Ritz.'

Krasin had stood up slowly, brushing his hand over his sparse hair.

'Let's go then before they come for us.'

She opened her mouth to speak and then changed her mind. There was little enough to collect, and half an hour later they were having coffee in the lounge of the Ritz while they waited for the hire-car to arrive.

By midday the débâcle in London was known in Moscow and already Andropov had instigated a harassment programme against the British Embassy.

Hoult had tried Adèle's number several times but there had been no response. He had telephoned Layton, who had promised to have the situation in Paris checked immediately.

Hoult had waited at the hotel with Yelena for Layton's contact call, and it was early evening before the phone rang. Adèle had not returned to her apartment and there was no indication that she had contacted any of her friends or her family. Layton had arranged for one of his men in Paris to see what he could find out.

'I'll have to go over and find out what has happened, Yelena.'

'You think tnese people will not be efficient?'

'It will be unimportant to them now they've got Soloviev and the others. There's so much going on at the moment that a missing Frenchwoman won't be all that important.'

'But it's important to you, Jamie?'

He sat down on the bed beside her. He spoke slowly as if he were thinking aloud. 'Even that isn't true. I feel very remote from Adèle. My life with her seems as far away as the war. I ought to feel more than I do, friendliness maybe, or sympathy, but I feel nothing except responsibility. She was a hostage because of me, for no other reason. Since we parted she has never intruded into my life, nor I into hers. But I *have* now. And although it was not my choosing it *is* my fault, so I must do what I can.'

'Can I come with you?'

'It would be much better if you stayed. Much safer too. But I should be desperately unhappy without you.'

'When shall we start?'

'I must make some arrangements and a few telephone calls. We'll leave early tomorrow.'

'Do you think they would harm her?'

'Depends on who it is. If it is just Krasin, then maybe not. If others were involved, then who knows?'

'Viktor always spoke of her with affection.'

'But he's still KGB, my love. He didn't protect you when the heat was on.'

'We'll see, Jamie. Let us hope for the best.'

He leaned over and kissed her, and for a moment rested his head on her shoulder. She watched him gather together his spirits as he sat down at the table and reached for the telephone. She felt terribly sad for him but there was little she could do. As with so many times in his life he was doing what circumstances made him do. That he would do it well she had no doubt, but that it would harm him she also had no doubt. Every man had his ration of courage and she knew that James Hoult's ration was almost at its end.

Hoult slept uneasily that night, and as he lay awake he remembered the first night with Yelena at the hotel in Moscow. All those feelings of doubt and insecurity were back again. Another hotel room, another crisis, but the same need for deciding the priorities, or working out what kind of man he was.

Kuznetsov had boarded the Aeroflot flight to de Gaulle just after 1 a.m. Layton's man now had a list of the de Massu properties, and had made some discreet enquiries of the SDECE at the Boulevard Mortier.

In London, editors were passing stop-press items for the last run of the final editions, envying their evening paper rivals who would be able to cover in full the PM's midnight declaration of a State of Emergency.

CHAPTER THIRTEEN

Adèle drove the white *deux-chevaux* with Krasin hunched up in the seat beside her. They had driven back to the Rue de la Huchette and had taken the sheets, blankets and pillows from the beds and food from the refrigerator. From the *quai* they had turned left into the Boulevard Saint-Michel. There was no traffic in the streets and they were quickly on to the M-13. By the time they were alongside the heliport Krasin was asleep. Adèle had cast a quick glance downriver as they swept across the flyover over the Seine. There was the first faint light of the dawn. There were workmen repairing the road in the Rue de la Reine and by the time they reached Sèvres a fine drizzle had cut down their speed.

By Nantes there was light enough to drive by, and at Louviers Sunday traffic was beginning to edge on to the motorway. At the big junction at Pont-Audemer the traffic was heavy, and she took the secondary road, alongside the railway, that led to Honfleur.

When she stopped the car at the yacht basin, Krasin still slept and she rested her head for a moment on the steering wheel. Then she opened the door gently and stepped out into the early morning sunshine. There were owners mopping down the decks of their cruisers, and although there seemed to be no wind there was the flapping of sheets on metal masts. As she watched, a Dutch yacht locked into the basin and slowly moved over to the temporary berths. Life was going on normally for all these people and she wondered what they would say if she told them why she was there. She wrapped the black silk evening coat around her and bent to look back in the car. She shook Krasin and as he opened his eyes he smiled as he saw her. Then she saw his memory of what had happened flood back, and he

147

shook his head and touched the rough stubble of his jaw. She had bought food and cigarettes, razor and blades, and a two-litre can of milk.

The cottage was out towards the estuary and as she turned into the open gate and down the long rutted path she could just see the cottage through the sea-mist.

In every large city there are districts with romantic-sounding names which imply a beauty that is seldom fulfilled. Belleville, in Paris, is one of these. In Belleville, industry stamps its dirty feet on steel and iron, young men dream of another May '68, and the local Communist Party has enough potential members to pick and choose. Two men it had chosen were father and son, Jacques and Alain Janin.

Kuznetsov and the two Janins sat in the small front parlour, whose dust-sheets had been removed in deference to their guest. Janin senior was a welder, and his son worked as a telephone operator on the international exchange. It was he who had telephoned the Embassy when the young man at the bookshop had tried, and failed, to contact Krasin at the apartment in the Rue de la Huchette.

Andropov's instructions to Kuznetsov had been simple and explicit. Find Krasin and the de Massu woman and put an end to them both. The Paris Embassy had been alerted to give cover, support and advice. Kuznetsov was young and tough but his French was poor and his forte was violence rather than diplomacy.

Alain Janin had checked the duty slips on calls to and from the apartment in the Rue de la Huchette, and Soloviev's late-night call was there. There had been no subsequent calls, either in or out. All other calls made in the last three days were logged and accounted for. A two-man team from the Soviet Embassy was carrying out surveillance on Adèle de Massu's apartment and a journalist had been paid to make discreet enquiries amongst the family's social circle. Kuznetsov was used to the facilities of the KGB, and he had to control his impatience with considerable effort at being an outsider in a foreign city, where his

148

influence was virtually non-existent and his resources pathetically limited.

Layton's man was an old hand from SOE. And now that he sold Jaguars, his pink ribbon of the Légion d'Honneur stood him in good stead. He was more at home in Paris than anywhere in England and his only concession to his compatriots was not to cheer for the French XV when England came to the Stade de Colombes. His cover with the Jaguar concession paid him handsomely, and Layton only used his time for special operations. His network into Paris business and society circles was the main reason for his present assignment.

He sat at the small neat desk with the telephone in front of him and the list of de Massu properties on his blotter. As Paul Beresford, with a superb second-hand XJ6 registered in 1970 available for just over 10,000 NF, he had all the excuse for contacting Adèle de Massu that he needed. He had supplied cars to the family for years and it was genuinely time for milady to abandon the old Mark IX, however pristine it might be.

For three hours he telephoned, but all he got was a blank. Nobody knew where she was. Nobody seemed particularly worried. Her boys were away so maybe she was taking a few days' holiday somewhere. Layton had cautioned him about arousing the suspicion of her parents but he couldn't see how he could get further without implying some urgent need.

After lunch there had been a call from one of his contacts at SDECE. A routine check of the Russian Embassy's activities had thrown up Adèle de Massu's name on a guest list for a concert. The concert was the day before Krasin had contacted Hoult. A further check had indicated a discrepancy in the number of official guests and the number of seats occupied by the Soviet party. There was a missing seat and Beresford guessed it might have been caused by Krasin's name being omitted from the official list. They wouldn't give him a cover name because there could be people there who knew him, they didn't want to use his real name for security reasons, so they just slipped him in as an extra. SDECE would like to be kept in touch.

He could try some of the embassy chauffeurs to see if any of them had seen the woman leave with Krasin, but that wouldn't get him far either. She *must* have left with Krasin. He needed to check over her apartment, and that meant a break-in, and he would need Layton's OK and some sort of deal with the police through SDECE.

He dialled the London duty number but Layton was not available. He decided to go ahead anyway. The trail was already getting cold and Layton had indicated that there may be others looking for the missing woman.

Hoult had booked them in at a small hotel just off the Rue des Capucines, with its old-fashioned entrance in the Place Vendôme. He had no leads, and no support, and he knew that his only recourse was the de Massu family. Her father had died just after the divorce, and her mother had not kept on the big town house. She had an apartment now, over one of the ornate shops in the Faubourg-St-Honoré.

She agreed to see him later that day and invited them both to tea. Hoult would have preferred to go alone but it would have been churlish to ignore the gesture that was meant to show a friendly impartiality. She had always seemed to like him, and had written him a gentle letter when it had all broken up.

The room was elegant and feminine, and she sat with her stick at her side, in a straight-backed chair, one of her legs on a small embroidered stool. She waved them to the seats opposite and pressed the bell on a side-table.

'We'll have one of your English teas, Jamie.'

She leaned stiffly forward towards Yelena, smiling and pushing back a wisp of loose hair. 'He used to come to see me sometimes when he was at the bank. He'd eat like a horse, you know. I always thought he was half-starved, living in that silly room across the river.' She signalled to the maid to put the tray down. When she had poured

150

their tea and handed it round she leaned back, and put her hand on her stick as if for moral support, she looked at Hoult.

'How can I help you, my dear?'

'I'm worried about Adèle, *maman*. I believe she's in danger.'

The old lady looked at him sharply, and he could see that she was confused. A social call was turning into an embarrassing situation. He went on quickly. 'A threat was made to me that unless I did what was required then Adèle would be in jeopardy.'

'And you have been to the police?'

'The authorities in London are taking action and I am sure they will inform their counterparts here in Paris.'

'So why have they not contacted me?'

'I expect it's because they don't want to cause alarm if it isn't necessary, and that they want to avoid any scandal.'

Scandal was a word the old lady understood. Great efforts could be made to avoid scandal. She shifted her stick uneasily.

'They asked you to come and tell me, Jamie?'

'No, I came because I wanted to help. But I need your help.'

'What help can I give, my dear?'

'I want your permission to look over Adèle's apartment to see if I can find some clue as to where she might be.'

She nodded. 'That is no problem, speak to Marie about a key when you go, she's got one somewhere. Is there anything else?'

'Is there anywhere she might stay that you know of?'

She half-smiled. 'I see her maybe once every two weeks. She never talks of her life. We just gossip, nothing more.'

She turned to Yelena. 'You look sad, my dear. Maybe you are afraid of all this with another wife. Let me console you.' She smiled, and the effort was obvious. 'He looks happier, even in this moment, than I ever saw him before. And that can only be you. It may be no consolation, but I have never heard my daughter say anything but good of

151

this man. She said you were very very beautiful and I can see she was right.'

But there was no good to be done in that direction, and the old lady sighed and struggled to stand up. The interview was over and she hobbled over to the inner door with them, as a gesture of her approval.

When they had gone she went back to her chair, and sat in the darkening room wondering how it all had gone so wrong.

It was nearly ten o'clock. Hoult walked from the main road to the Rue du Sentier and then turned left into a small cobbled courtyard. It was not far from the place they had had when he was first married, and as he stood there, he wondered if that was why Adèle had come back here. He saw her house immediately, the bright blue shutters, the pelargoniums, the lobelia and alyssum, all spoke of Adèle. The pale green leaves of the two young plane trees looked transparent in the light of the street lamp.

There was no sound in the little yard, apart from the distant hum of the Paris traffic, and Hoult was conscious of a feeling of great peace. Adèle's apartment was upstairs, and had its own entrance facing the square.

The key turned easily and he walked inside. There was a smell of apples on the stairs and as he switched on the light he saw a photograph of the boys on the wall. He stood and looked at the picture. It must have been taken some years back – Piers with his big, serious eyes and tight, curly hair, and Blair looking under his eyelids trying not to laugh. The handrail of the stairs was worn smooth, and in the narrow siting-room there were more photographs, including a studio portrait of himself in a silver frame.

It seemed an indecency to be in Adèle's home, behind her back, with all the evidence of her life displayed so artlessly. There was a Louis Seize escritoire, and he lowered its front panel and pulled out the slides. There were pigeon-holes with neat bundles of receipts and statements. Letters from friends and relatives, concert and theatre programmes, and insurance documents in plastic cases. The long top drawer was crowded with writing paper and the paraphernalia of correspondence. In the second was a document with pink tape. It was her will and he was tempted to look. There was a diary bound in leather with a light brass latch and lock but no sign of a key.

There were four bookshelves in an alcove and he looked idly for a few moments at their titles. They were all twaddle, women's stuff, except for some historical biographies. There was almost nothing in English, except some tattered Biggles paperbacks and half a dozen school books.

He walked slowly round the room. It was entirely a woman's room. Elegant, tasteful, but with evidence here and there of childishness rather than youthfulness. And then he was suddenly ashamed of the pettiness of his thoughts about a woman who might be in danger because of his actions.

There were no clues of any kind in the simple bedroom, the only papers were a copy of the French edition of *Vogue* and a folded copy of *Illustrated London News* still in its postal wrapper.

He went back to the escritoire and sat down. There was a small note-pad with shopping lists and phone numbers, and he had left the leather diary lying at the side of a pile of bills. He touched a thumb-nail to the diary lock but it didn't give. He couldn't bring himself, as yet, to break it open. He went through the pigeon-holes again but there was nothing. He realized that he had no idea what he was looking for. What could there be that was likely to provide a clue to where she could be? He stood up slowly and walked across to the window. He wished that Yelena was with him but it hadn't seemed right to bring her. The small square was gold from the light of the street lamp and on the edge of the pool of light he saw a man who stood looking up at the window. As Hoult watched, the man walked slowly towards the building. Hoult heard the doorbell ring a few seconds later. As he hesitated it rang again, impatiently.

He opened the door and the man was leaning against the wall, a cigarette in his mouth. Hoult was conscious of being carefully examined, and as he opened his mouth to speak the man said, 'You must be Hoult.'

'Who are you?'

'My name's Beresford, I'm a friend of Layton; it would be more sensible if I came in.'

'You're English?'

'Welsh.'

Hoult stood aside and Beresford walked up the stairs as Hoult closed the door behind them. In the sitting-room he stood in the middle of the room, his eyes taking in the layout. He turned to Hoult and his eyes glanced towards the bedroom.

'She's not here, I suppose?'

'No.'

'Any indications where she might be? You picked up anything?'

'Not a thing.'

Beresford sat at the escritoire and pulled out all the papers. He picked up the diary. 'Have you found a key to this?'

'No.'

He opened the drawers and pushed everything around and then walked over to the small kitchen and came back with a knife. He slid the blade under the catch and moved it from side to side and then pressed downwards. The lock gave, and broke at the hinge. Beresford lit a cigarette and turned the pages and read back through the diary. After ten minutes he closed it and pushed it aside. He looked over the papers and reached for the note-pad.

'Have you checked these telephone numbers?'

'No.'

Beresford reached for the telephone and made space for it in front of him. He looked at the pad and dialled a number. There was no answer. The second number was a restaurant and then there were two more blanks.

He pulled a thin blue book from his inside pocket, opened it, and holding it open he dialled again. He asked for an Inspector Mollet and asked him to check a list of telephone numbers. He gave Adèle's number and said he would wait.

He put the phone down and for the next ten minutes he searched the apartment, thoroughly and professionally. When he had finished he made himself comfortable in an armchair and lifted the phone from the desk and put it between his feet.

'Have you contacted Layton since you came over, Sir James?'

'No, I came unofficially.'

'Where are you staying?'

'At the Hotel Duval on the Rue des Capucines.'

'Are you alone?'

'No, my wife is with me.'

'And you're looking for Adèle de Massu?'

'Yes.'

The phone rang. Beresford lifted the receiver and listened, carefully making notes on the pad. When he put down the phone he looked at the notes, and said slowly as he read, 'This could be promising, a lawyer. Let's try him first. Jouvet – Charles Jouvet. He's out at Neuilly.'

He dialled and leaned back. 'Monsieur Jouvet?'

'Speaking.'

'Ah, *monsieur*, I'm trying to contact Adèle de Massu. I understand she was in touch with you recently. Maybe you could put me in touch.'

'Who is that?'

'My name's Beresford. I have the Jaguar agency near the United States Embassy. However I'm calling on behalf of Sir James Hoult who was previously her husband. There is some urgent private matter, I understand.'

'I'm afraid I cannot help you. Have you tried her apartment?'

155

'Yes, of course. Sir James and I are here now.'

'You have permission to be there?'

'Just a moment, *monsieur*. Have we permission to be here, Sir James?' He waited.

'Her mother gave permission and supplied a key.'

'Yes *monsieur*, Madame de Massu gave permission and a key.'

'Good, good. However I still cannot help you.'

'May I ask, *monsieur*, what was involved when Adèle de Massu contacted you?'

'I'm afraid that is confidential. However, I can say that it could have no relevance.'

'Would you allow me to be the judge of that, *monsieur*?'

'Most definitely not. You should know better than that.'

'Would it help if I asked Inspector Mollet to contact you? But I would prefer to keep it private if possible.'

There were a few moments of silence. 'This is really most irregular; I think you had better come to my office tomorrow.'

'*Monsieur*, can I speak in confidence to you?'

'I could not commit myself.'

'It is possible that Adèle de Massu has been put under pressure for political reasons. I am acting for the appropriate authorities as adviser to the family.'

'I see. I was consulted on a very minor matter. I was asked to check the lease of a holiday cottage. It was quite in order. That, I'm afraid, was all.'

'Where was the cottage?'

'At Honfleur.'

'Can you remember the address?'

'Yes. A moment while I think. It was Ferme des ... something. To do with the weather or the sea. Yes, that's it, Ferme des Brumes.'

'Did she take it?'

'That I don't know. I had the feeling she intended to go ahead but she would do that with the owners.'

'Was that a Madame Saint Clair by any chance?'

'Yes. I think it was.'

'Thank you very much, *monsieur*.'

'Not at all.'

Beresford dialled another number and nodded at Hoult as it rang. 'I think we're on the move. Ah, good evening, may I speak to Madame Saint Clair?'

'A moment.'

'Juliette Saint Clair. Who is that?'

'*Madame*, I am enquiring about your cottage at Honfleur. I understood from Adèle de Massu that she was taking it for a few months. If she does not, then I would be interested.'

'Oh yes, but I'm afraid that she has taken it until September. I am so sorry. However I have another cottage at Lisieux if you would be interested.'

'I had set my heart on Honfleur, *madame*. Where exactly is it situated?'

'You know Honfleur?'

'I'm afraid not.'

'Well you leave the town to the north by the public gardens and go along past the West Digue, and four miles on you turn left at an old barn and then you see a post fence and a path. There is the cottage.

'Thank you so much, *madame*.'

'Good night.'

Beresford put the phone down slowly. 'That's where they'll be, Sir James. And it means she must have some control over the situation. I can't understand why Krasin didn't release her on Soloviev's orders but that's water under the bridge. I suggest that I go out there immediately and see if I can spot them. There's no point in you going right now. If they saw you it could raise problems. Maybe when we get a picture of what's going on you could be really useful. We've got a lot of problems anyway in this situation.'

'What particular problems?'

'Layton has no jurisdiction over Krasin or your former wife. They are foreigners in a foreign country. Whatever Krasin and the Russians are up to they are now the problem of the French authorities.'

Hoult had reluctantly agreed and Beresford had taken his address and telephone number at the hotel. He had promised to keep in touch.

It was nearly ten o'clock when Beresford parked his car. He sat over his breakfast looking over the Place Ste-Catherine. There were already the first small groups of visitors looking at the old church. The impatient axe-masters of Honfleur had built their church of wood to thank their God for peace, and the departure of the English, after the Hundred Years War. And now, the sun enriched the texture and made the dark wood glow. It was going to be a hot day and extra tables were being arranged at the edge of the square.

He had asked for a telephone directory and had sat looking through for the name St Clair, but there was no entry. There was probably no phone installed.

He had a poor photocopy of an old photograph of Adèle de Massu, but only a verbal description of Krasin; and he tried to imagine what was happening at the cottage as he drove slowly down the road alongside the jetty. Soon the houses grew sparser and the road twisted and turned across the flat, open landscape. Half a mile beyond the barn he left the car and started walking. The heat mist lay in patches across the fields and the heavy Normandy cattle stood idly grazing in the lush meadows, their white, panda-like faces turning slowly towards him as he skirted the dry-stone walls that kept them from the mud flats. He came on the fence, and the sagging open gate, sooner than he expected.

There was no sign of the cottage, and the white mist lay thick across a sparse orchard of apple trees whose stunted, twisted branches bespoke the sins of absentee owners. He tried the binoculars but it was pointless, it was the mist not distance that hid the cottage.

Almost an hour later he could see the faint outline of the cottage and he entered the orchard and lay prone behind one of the gnarled trees and trained his glasses on the long, low building. It was solid stone and built to resist invaders as well as the winter storms of Normandy. The windows and door were closed, and nothing stirred in the silence.

He lay for two hours in the damp grass before there was any movement. It was the woman, and he recognized her at once as she walked across to an open barn, and he saw the small car as she swung back the big doors. There was no air about her of being a prisoner and she walked back to a seat at the side of the door and arranged her hair with her head against the wall.

Then Krasin came out, he recognized him, the description had been accurate. He said something to the woman as he leaned, relaxed, against the door. And she looked up at him, laughing as she spoke. There was obviously no force involved in their relationship, unless some other pressure than physical force had been applied.

According to Layton and Hoult, Krasin had been Adèle's kidnapper and gaoler, but he had also been ordered by Soloviev to release her. And according to the French authorities' records Krasin had never entered the country. This tangled little web was for Layton to unravel.

He had worked his way back to the wall and along to the open five-barred gate. Nobody passed him on his way back to the car. He drove through Honfleur and took the road south to Barneville and booked a room at l'Auberge de la Source. It took him an hour to contact Layton and he was told to wait for further instructions while SIS liaised with the SDECE in Paris.

Layton came back on the telephone after an hour. The French were passing the buck between SDECE and their internal security rivals the DTS. The issue would not be decided until early the next day. Neither of the two security forces wanted to get stuck with Krasin. The French *détente* with Moscow had top priority at the Quai d'Orsay, apart from which, nobody had suggested that Krasin was operating against the French. Why should the French security services pick the SIS chestnuts out of the fire? Layton had hinted in a roundabout way that if they kept stalling he would order Beresford to make direct contact with Adèle de Massu at the cottage. The last little problem was that it wasn't clear from the records whether or not Adèle de Massu had retained, or given up, her British nationality that came with her marriage to Hoult. So did SIS have even that tenuous jurisdiction? It was shaping up for one of those fierce international snarling matches that never make the press but do their damage quietly underground for years. Like Sapphire and the CIA, when a Russian KGB defector had named ten Frenchmen as Soviet agents, four of whom were French representatives at NATO and the others were at the top of the SDECE.

He phoned through to Hoult and gave him only brief details of the position and tried to reassure him that everything was under control.

A man from the SDECE phoned a special number at the Soviet Embassy in London. Ten minutes later a short-wave encyphered message went by radio to the Soviet Embassy in Paris. The ambassador was at a special performance of *Phèdre* at the Théâtre de France and a KGB major was despatched to join his chauffeur who had been allowed to park the car in the Luxembourg Gardens. But it was midnight before His Excellency had left the reception at the theatre. He read the message on his way back to the Embassy and the major was given his instructions. He had parked his car near the Belleville Métro Station and walked through the narrow streets to the house.

He stood on the narrow doorstep with his finger on the bell push. He knew all too well that at two in the morning people tended to sleep as if they were drugged. It was several minutes before a light went on in the upstairs rooms. He could hear the clatter of loose shoes on naked feet as someone came slowly down the stairs. A rough voice said 'Qui est là?' and he said softly 'Les amis de la France'. There was a long pause and then the chain rattled as it was unhooked. The old man looked him over carefully, his mouth gaping, and he shuffled back and beckoned him inside.

Kuznetsov had sat shivering in his shirt and trousers as he listened to his instructions. Finally the man from the Embassy handed over the Ordnance Survey maps, the Luger, and three boxes of cartridges.

Kuznetsov sat alone, stripping and checking the Luger. It was the short PO8 and the cartridges were jacketed with zinc over a lead core. Lethal, but not first-time 'stoppers', you could hit a man and he could still kill you before he died. He wished they'd issued him with a revolver and those big, soft, fast bullets that went through a man like a mincer. He took the stuff upstairs with him and went back to sleep. It was going to be a long day tomorrow and he wanted to be on form. He had killed men before but always close-up and unarmed. As his eyes closed he wished that he had listened more carefully at the small arms school.

Yelena had listened as Hoult talked with Beresford. It seemed like some opera plot to think of Krasin and Adèle together in some lonely cottage near the sea. Her instinct was that there was no danger. And being a woman, and knowing Krasin, she wondered if he had bedded down her husband's first wife. It would, in a senseless, outrageous sort of way, complete the circle. Everybody would have slept with everybody.

She was pleased that Hoult seemed to come out of his oppressive cloud of responsibility.

He had taken her to a small restaurant and had seemed to be almost light-hearted as they talked while they ate.

'Are you happy again, Jamie?'

He smiled and reached across to touch her hand.

'I feel now that it's coming to an end. Adèle will be free, if she isn't already free, and my responsibility will be over.'

'Shall you see her?'

He put his head on one side and suddenly she was back in Moscow and he was talking about Glasgow working-men. Defending their drunkenness.

161

'We will go down to Honfleur tomorrow and when Beresford goes to the cottage we'll check that all is well, and then we'll go away for a few weeks and decide where to live.'

'Not back to England?'

He shook his head and avoided her eyes. 'No. My solicitor can clear up things for us there. Where would you like to live?'

She smiled. 'Could we stay in France, my love?'

'It would be sensible with your good French. And where should we live in France?'

'I could be very happy here in Paris.'

His fingers gently stroked her hand. 'And so you shall, my love. And so you shall.'

They had walked down to the Pont St-Michel and the floodlights had turned Notre-Dame into a wedding cake. She stood alongside him, leaning on the parapet of the bridge, his arm around her shoulders and hers around his waist. There is a day in early spring when the first fat bumblebees appear, and a day in late September when red admirals and peacocks lie on Michaelmas daisies and buddleia as if it were some saint's day to mark the end of the summer, and in every love affair there is a moment in one day that seals the lovers' fates. From that day on the dice are cast, and from that moment on they will be a couple, cast in some good metal, like a statue, their separate lives are fused inevitably. It has nothing to do with making love, or marriage, and it may have nothing to do with happiness, because it sometimes happens in the joint grief of a lost child. And in such a moment their faces turned towards each other, without a smile, without a kiss, but knowing that they would remember this bridge and this night for the rest of their lives.

CHAPTER FOURTEEN

Beresford had listened to the BBC news at eight o'clock. The State of Emergency would end at midnight. The clockwork communists in the trade-unions had failed in their attempts to call a general strike. The mass of trade-unionists had had enough. Two Cabinet Ministers had resigned and the PM had accepted their letters of resignation before he received them. The BBC television programmes which had been 'blacked' for twenty-four hours would be back on the screens by midday. The pound had risen overnight on the New York market to an almost unbelievable $2.50 and Boycott had been nominated as captain of the final Test match against the Australians.

Just after ten o'clock Layton had telephoned. Neither the SDECE or the Direction de la Sécurité du Territoire would touch Krasin with a barge-pole. If SIS wanted to take some action a blind eye would be turned. If he had made an illegal entry then let him be picked up in the normal checks by the police. So far as Adèle de Massu was concerned, she had become a British subject by marriage and was of no concern to either French security force.

Layton had spoken off the record to the SDECE representative in London who had gone over to watch the SIS operation against the subversives. He had smiled a knowing smile and pointed out that the French Minister for Industry was in Moscow at the moment, for the signing of a trade contract worth 500 billion francs. Layton had said, 'Go very carefully, Beresford. Try and keep clear of the local police. Our obligation goes no further than checking that the woman is free to leave if she wants to. Offer to escort her back to Paris if you have any doubt.'

'Do I keep Hoult himself in the picture?'

'I suppose so. Just the bare facts. Give every impression

163

of a friendly reception back here, and check his movements until he's on his way back.'

'Are you picking him up?'

'Too bloody true we are. He's going inside with the rest of them.'

Adèle de Massu was a lady, but not so much of a lady that there wasn't some subconscious satisfaction that Krasin's lovemaking had balanced the books. That wasn't, even vaguely, one of the reasons for accepting his advances. It had happened quite naturally that first night at the cottage, when they were both suddenly aware of a feeling of euphoria at escaping from the tension of their situation in Paris. The fact that he couldn't wait until she was undressed was flattering at forty, and as if he had been her lover all her life he aroused her in a way that her husband had never done.

She looked at him now, as he slept. The wavy hair, the full mouth, and the lined face, undoubtedly made a handsome whole. He looked amused and sophisticated even when he slept. There was a hint of Charles Boyer when he had played Pépé le Moko. He stirred as she watched him and as his head turned, a shaft of sunlight from the shutters touched his face, and he slowly opened his eyes. He smiled slowly as she looked at him, and with a satisfying responsiveness he reached for her, and as she lay along his body she leaned up to let him kiss the tips of her breasts. She sighed with pleasure as he went in her and for an hour he had had her without inhibition, and she was erotically aware that it was her urgent, vulgar words that prolonged her excitement. There was no thought of James Hoult in her mind as she clung frenziedly to the man from Moscow.

At midday they had eaten and, as had become their habit, they walked in the hot sun towards the mud-flats that led towards the sea. A thousand small streams were running after the ebbing tide, and as they walked shoe-less the sun turned the sand and the mud into rippling waves of gold and silver.

164

Krasin had looked at her, aware of her beauty and the new sparkle in her eyes, and felt that maybe there *was* survival here in France. She smiled up at him like a school-girl in love.

'Tell me what you're thinking, Viktor.'

'I wondered how difficult it would be for us to stay. And if I would get work.'

'There'll be no problems, no problems at all. You have great talent, wide experience and we have influence, you know. The bank finances films, and dabbles extravagantly in all the arts. You just leave it to me.'

Adèle de Massu was already wondering whether the uncle twice removed who was the Bishop of Angoulême would enable her to be married a second time in white.

Getting a cycle into the back of a Fiat 500 involved loosening the handle-bar head-lock ring or *la tête de fourche* as it said in the instruction book, and a considerable amount of pushing and shoving.

Kuznetsov's car had broken down twice on the long journey from Paris. He had had to pay for a new fan-belt and, on the second break-down, for new contacts. He was an hour later than he planned so he drove without stopping through Honfleur and parked just beyond the *digue* on the north side of the town.

He sat in the car eating his sandwiches and drinking from a can of beer. He turned on the radio and tried to follow the news from Paris-Inter, but his French only worked when he could throw in a bit of sign-language as reinforcement. But he caught the words *Londres* and *Moscou* and *provocateurs* enough times to realize that the operation in England was not going too well. He tuned along the dial but there was nothing in any language that he could understand. He pressed the button to change the wavelength and listened to the BBC. They had finished the main news and were giving the headlines again. For the first time in three days he was glad that he was not in Moscow. Andropov must be getting hell from the Politburo.

They had recalled the London Ambassador 'for consultations' and the Leningrad Symphony Orchestra had been recalled from its six weeks' tour after only one concert.

He emptied all the cartridges from the boxes and cleaned them carefully and thoroughly with an oily rag. He loaded the magazine and snapped it back up into the stock. He lifted the toggle and heard the first cartridge drive into the breech.

For the last time he went over the large-scale map, and measured again the distance from the barn to the gate, and from the gate to the cottage. He looked idly across to the sea and it stirred his mind so that his hand went to his inside pocket to pull out the plastic envelope. They had given him another twenty-four hours, and then he was to make his way to Le Havre and use the seaman's documents to join a Soviet timber ship that was unloading at the port.

They were almost back at the cottage when she stopped him and looked up at his face. 'Shall we go back to Paris tomorrow? You can stay at my place while I get your papers fixed.'

'And then?'

She said very softly, 'You can stay until you want to go.'

He looked at her and put his hand on her shoulder, his fingers touching her slender neck. 'You know what you're saying, Adèle.'

'Yes, I know.'

'And your mother, and your friends?'

'You'll be welcome, Viktor. Don't worry. We'll be just like any other couple. I feel alive again.'

He sighed. 'You mustn't be hurt again.'

'Will you hurt me, then?'

He shook his head and smiled. 'No. I'll never hurt you.'

'Let's go back.'

Back at the cottage they had planned and talked as they sat with a bottle of wine and Krasin had gone into the dim light of the bedroom. He lay facing the windows watching

166

the ivy leaves make shadows on the shutters as they twisted in the light sea-breeze. It was all so quiet, all so still, and all so beautiful. And he closed his eyes and slept.

Kuznetsov had cursed as he wrenched the cycle from the back seat of the car and when he had tightened and adjusted the handlebars he swung his leg over and headed for the barn where he turned left, and then right at the bottom of the rough road. He didn't turn his head as he passed the gate to the cottage and continued along the road until it rose up gradually to the foot of a gently sloping hill. And there he propped the cycle against the stone wall and sat on the hillside to light a cigarette. He looked first across the mud-flats to the sea, and then, watching a gull, he turned so that he could see the cottage. The door was ajar but there was no sign of people inside it.

He watched and waited for almost an hour, and then he saw a man. He had stopped at the barn, then turned to walk along the front of the cottage. He walked in through the open blue door and Kuznetsov moved back to his cycle.

Hoult had been reassured when they had found the barn, and as he closed the door of the car he leaned inside to kiss Yelena. 'I'll be straight back my love, don't worry.'

He walked in the hot sun, the dust of the road leaving a trail behind him. Where the road turned he swung round and waved to Yelena, and then he was lost to sight as the ground sloped away.

Grass grew over the bottom bar of the leaning gate. It certainly had not been used for months. The sun was on his back and he saw the bumper of a small car where it reflected a splash of light. The front of the cottage was covered with ivy and virginia creeper, just beginning to show signs of colour. The blue door stood ajar, and there was an old wooden seat alongside it. He wondered if they had watched him walk down the path.

At the door he hesitated, then pushed it slowly aside

and walked in. Away from the sunlight the square room was shadowy, and then he heard the rattle of crockery from what must be the kitchen. A moment later Adèle had walked in, a loaf of bread in her hand. She stood there with her eyes wide, and her mouth open in shock.

'It's only me, Adèle. I came to see that you were all right.'

She closed her eyes and sighed so heavily he thought she was going to faint. But she moved slowly to the table and put down the loaf. Still looking at him she said, 'Oh, Jamie, you seemed like a ghost. For a moment I was frightened.'

He smiled gently, making no move towards her. 'And are you all right?'

'Oh yes. He wouldn't do what they said.'

'Where is Viktor?'

She nodded her head towards the closed door. 'He's in there, Jamie. He's asleep.'

'What happened?'

'He had a telephone message from a Russian in London. The message said I was to be freed. But he used some sort of codeword to say he was under pressure. And that meant he *must* kill me.'

'So?'

'He's not a killer, Jamie. He's on the run. I shall help him all I can.'

'And you? How about you?'

'I'm fine, there's ...' And there was a swath of sunshine from the door behind him and he saw Adèle's eyes dilate with fear. Her mouth opened to shout and her hand came up as if to fend off some blow, and that was the last thing he ever saw. Two bullets ripped into his back, and one into the base of his skull.

Beresford had pulled up his car alongside Hoult's and he recognized Yelena at once from the description. He walked over and bent down to speak to her.

'I think you must be Lady Hoult, madam.'

'Yes, who are you?'

'I'm a friend of your husband's. My name is Beresford. Where is he at the moment?'

She felt suddenly faint with apprehension and she said in a whisper. 'He's walked down to the cottage.'

'Is he alone?'

'Yes. He asked me to wait.'

'I think perhaps you should come with me. I'm going down there myself. We could . . .' And in the stillness of the hot summer evening six shots had ripped out. A burst of three and then another three.

'Christ! Move over please.' He fumbled for the ignition, started the engine, and the tyres spun as he swung the car down the road and through the open gate. They were half-way to the cottage when a man came running from it. He was barefoot and naked to the waist, his face was white and contorted. As they pulled up he collapsed and fell to the ground. Beresford jumped out and knelt beside him. The man had struggled to lean up and for a moment he pointed to the cottage and said, 'Oh, Mother of God! Mother of God!' and then fell back. Beresford shouted to Yelena as he ran, 'Stay there. Don't get out. Don't move.' And he pulled out a gun from inside his jacket.

The door was wide open and Hoult's body lay face down, his arms outstretched towards the woman. Adèle de Massu had taken a bullet in her mouth and one between her eyes and one at the base of her neck. The one at her neck had churned open on entering, and her clothes were red-wet where the bright arterial blood had jetted out.

He searched the cottage. In cupboards, under the beds, every room, and he had circled the building twice and checked the barn and the car. There was nobody else there. The man who had run out must be Krasin. He must have killed Hoult. But why? Hoult would never have brought along his wife if he intended any violence to Krasin. Maybe Krasin had panicked. Or maybe . . . and he walked back quickly to the cottage. He bent over the woman's body and pulled back her skirt. After a few moments he re-

169

arranged her. He walked back up the rutted path. The girl was kneeling alongside Krasin wiping his face with a small handkerchief. He stood alongside them and as Krasin looked up at him he said, 'I assume you are Viktor Krasin?' The man nodded. 'You'd better come back with me. Into the cottage.'

He had supported the man as he stumbled along, and the girl had gone into the cottage before he had thought to stop her. He heard her cry out and he shoved Krasin towards the bedroom.

Yelena was kneeling by Hoult's body, her hand stroking his head. She was shaking her head slowly and through her sobs she was saying something in Russian. It sounded like a prayer.

He bent down beside her and reached over for her hand. Her eyes were closed and tears streamed down her cheeks as she went on with the words she was saying. When she opened her eyes she looked at his face. 'Was it Krasin?'

'I'm almost certain it wasn't. I think he was asleep in the bedroom at the time.'

She nodded. 'But it *was* the Russians.'

'Almost certainly.'

He put pressure gently under her arm so that she stood up as he did. She was trembling, and the full soft red lips quivered. The blue eyes turned to look at his face and she said softly, 'When will you people learn about these pigs in Moscow?'

'Some of us learnt a long time ago, Lady Hoult.'

'What will happen now? About Jamie, I mean.'

'There will be some formalities but I will deal with these if you will allow me to.'

'He will be buried properly? In a church place, I mean.'

'Of course. I think it would be best if he were buried near here.'

She nodded and the tears flowed again. As he watched she reached behind her neck and then she held out her cupped hand to him. There was a thin gold chain and a sovereign in a heap in her palm.

'I want this to be with him.'

It poured into his hand, and still looking at her he slid it into his pocket.

'I think you know Krasin well, Lady Hoult?'

She nodded without speaking.

'He's going to have problems. We shall try to do a deal with the people in Moscow but he's going to be a very disturbed man for a long time. Would you help him during the next few days?'

She sighed and looked towards the window.

'Yes. I'll help him.'

She walked with him as he turned to go into the bedroom. Krasin was recovering from his shock but he was beginning to shake. Beresford wrapped a blanket round him despite the furnace-like heat of the room.

'Tell me what happened.'

'I was asleep. I heard shots. I thought it was in my dream and then I came to look, to find Adèle. And they were there.'

'Was Hoult there before you went to sleep?'

'No. We were quite alone.'

'Did you hear anyone come, or leave?'

'No. I swear I heard nothing but the shots.'

'How many shots did you hear?'

'Two or three.'

'Did you look for a weapon?'

'No. I just panicked and ran out.'

'Where were you going?'

'To find help.'

'Where?'

'Oh God, I don't know. Anywhere.'

'Have you got a gun, Krasin?'

'Yes.'

'Where is it?'

'In my jacket.'

'And where is that?'

He looked around in a daze and then pointed to a wicker chair in the corner. 'There. On the chair.'

Beresford walked over and tried the pockets. There was a Walther PPK. He sniffed at the nose but there was nothing. He pressed the chamber release and slid out the magazine. It was full, and there was even grey fluff trapped in the flat spring. He took out all the cartridges. They were bone dry and dull, and so was the sear and the firing pin. It hadn't been fired for months. It hadn't been cared for, and it hadn't been in an armoury for years. No killer would carry a gun in such a state.

Beresford left them and walked back to the barn and checked the tyres of the *deux-chevaux*. Practically bald. Probably a hire-car. He walked back to his own car and then forward slowly checking the imprints on the sand. He traced the cycle tracks to the cottage door and then followed them back to the gate. The tracks ran both ways. It was something for the police. He walked back to the cottage, churning it over in his mind.

Krasin had dressed and was combing his hair. The tan was back on his face.

'Have either of you used a cycle since you've been here?'

Krasin shook his head. 'We don't ... didn't, have a cycle.'

'Anyone deliver anything for you – milk, groceries, anything like that?'

'Nobody came.'

'Somebody came today. What was in this code message about Adèle de Massu?'

'I had orders to kill her and the code in the message confirmed that.'

'Why didn't you carry out your orders?'

Krasin shrugged. 'I couldn't. I couldn't do it. So we came down here.'

Beresford sighed. He had promised his family he would be back tonight and there was a lot of clearing up to do.

'What were you planning to do, Mr Krasin?'

'I was going to get papers and stay in Paris. To try and get a job.'

'And now?'

'The same. I have no choice.'

Beresford nodded and turned to Yelena. 'Can you drive the car you came in, Lady Hoult?'

'I think so.'

'Right. Go to my car and take it back to where your own car was parked. Leave mine there, and take your own car. Go through Honfleur, and back down the road about four kilometres. Follow the signpost to Barneville-la Bertran. Go to l'Auberge de la Source. Use my name there, and book in for a week. I'll see you about eight or nine tonight.'

Yelena had stood up and made for the door, and Beresford called out, 'Mr Krasin will follow in a moment.' She nodded and left them, and she walked slowly and uncertainly as if she were drugged.

'Just one more question, Krasin. Have you been having sex with Adèle de Massu?'

'That would be ungallant to say.'

'So was threatening her life, mister. Just answer me yes or no.'

'Yes.'

'Today?'

'Yes.'

'OK. You'd better get on your way. Don't move out of your room till I come.'

Beresford had found five of the cartridge cases. They all had Czech manufacture marks. He walked back to his car and drove into Honfleur. From a public telephone kiosk he phoned Inspector Mollet. One of the blessings of a near-dictatorship is that things can be 'arranged'. Mollet had listened without interruption and then outlined what he referred to as the 'parameters of decision'. They had no intention of adding to Moscow's current embarrassments, so Krasin could be documented and dusted down so that he could earn a living. In case the Russians decided that having killed the wrong man they had better complete the job, the Quai d'Orsay would have a word in the Soviet Ambassador's accommodating ear. The present Lady

173

Hoult was a British subject and she could stay or return. Whatever she wished. So far as Hoult and Adèle de Massu were concerned, it was a matter for London. So far as the SDECE was concerned she was still British. His personal recommendation was a brief inquest at Honfleur. Open verdict. Hint of suicide pact. Not even a nine-days wonder if they played it right. There was enough news for the British media at the moment, and this wouldn't rate more than a couple of paragraphs. It was up to Layton.

Back at l'Auberge de la Source Beresford had waited impatiently for Layton's reply. It was nearly eleven before he called back. They would go along with Mollet's plan.

He had spent less than five minutes explaining the situation to Krasin and Lady Hoult, and they had been too exhausted, mentally and physically, to comment. Layton had said that if Lady Hoult required to move assets to another country it would be arranged without formalities.

He walked back down the corridor to his own room and lay on the bed. He took off his tie and loosened the collar of his shirt. His head touched the soft pillows and as his eyes closed he wondered how bastards like Hoult always got the pretty ones. The girl's face, the blue eyes, the snub nose, the full sexy mouth seemd to hang in his mind, and he had visions of those long, long legs. Maybe she would need a man and then he could ... And he slept.

Hoult had been buried in the cemetery at Honfleur. His sons had flown back from California, there had been half a dozen men she didn't recognize, and that was all. She had been driven back to the hotel at Pont-l'Evêque where Krasin was waiting for her.

They were staying for a few days at the Aigle d'Or in the Rue de Vaucelles. Krasin had his papers, and he had zeen offered a job at ORTF. He had had long interviews with the two French security services and they had taken a soft line in return for just a few names and a mite or two of background information. But despite all this he seemed to live in a fog of depression. As each practical difficulty was solved for him, the more he relied on her for his inner security.

That evening, after dinner, they had walked across the fields, along the hedgerows, and by the side of a stream they had sat looking at a field of corn. Without looking at her he had said to her, 'Will you stay with me, Yelena?'

She touched his hand where it rested on the dry grass. 'I'll stay with you, Viktor.'

He picked long stems of grass, touching the sharp edges with his fingertips. 'We're like survivors from some terrible war where everyone died except us. Only you and I know what happened. There is no one else we can ever talk to.'

He turned to look at her face, and she was conscious of a truth that he didn't know. He was all she had left of Jamie Hoult.